Double Teenage

Double Teenage
Joni Murphy

BookThug
Department of Narrative Studies
Toronto, 2016

SECOND PRINTING

LIBRARY AND ARCHIVES CANADA CATALOGUING IN PUBLICATION

Murphy, Joni, 1980–, author
        Double teenage / Joni Murphy.

Issued in print and electronic formats.
paperback: ISBN 978-1-77166-213-0
html: ISBN 978-1-77166-211-6
pdf: ISBN 978-1-77166-212-3
mobi: ISBN 978-1-77166-210-9

        I. Title.

PS3563.U74D68 2016   813'.54   C2016-900639-5
                                                     C2016-900640-9

PRINTED IN CANADA

Shelfie
A **bundled** eBook edition is available
with the purchase of this print book.

CLEARLY PRINT YOUR NAME ABOVE IN UPPER CASE
Instructions to claim your eBook edition:
1. Download the Shelfie app for Android or iOS
2. Write your name in **UPPER CASE** above
3. Use the Shelfie app to submit a photo
4. Download your eBook to any device

Friendship is not about having everything illuminated or obscured, but about conspiring and playing with shadows. Its goal is not enlightenment but luminosity, not a quest for the blinding truth but only for occasional lucidity and honesty.

—Svetlana Boym

It was very early in the morning.
Like radios, opiates, the groin's endless currency and surreptitious edge, buildings torn out of earth and forgotten.
Light could be tasted, had an odour like a tin can.
Girlhood is a landscape.
Across the morning earth, the pangs of a dying economy.

It was 1993.

—Lisa Robertson

1.

No Country for Young Girls

1.

In the valley ran a river. Their small city grew along one stretch. It was the river that made life there liveable, that let ancient people grow corn, squash, and beans for food and let others later grow cotton, chili, and pecans for cash. On one bank lay the edge of a rich country and on the other the edge of a poor one. Around the river was all this desert, a frayed cloth.

Theirs was a small city of inner endlessness without a center.

Three red crosses on a yellow background made the official city symbol. The crosses appeared in many forms, on the newspaper's masthead and as a little logo on the envelope of the water bill. In the downtown plaza three towered in rusting steel as so-called public art her mother hated. A sullen boy in after-school art class told Celine it was the symbol because conquistadors had lined colonial roads with crucified Indians.

"That's not true," her mother said, but even so the image fixed itself in Celine's head.

Sometimes sun reflected off car windows even as rain fell, and when the clouds opened for real, flash floods dug arroyos. Still the drought was entering its twentieth year. Neither mushrooms nor moss grew here. Life never sopped. Barbs guarded the smallest shoot. The most common plant was creosote bush, which looked the same dead or alive.

Water was status symbol. Turquoise kidney pools dotted subdivision backyards. Kids on swim teams screamed for fundraiser car washes in parking lots. They sent hose sprays down storm drains while the arid air dried their tropical-print towels in an instant. Rich growers flooded their pecan orchards in spring. This was a land of all nuance or none, it was just hard to tell which.

"We're actually better off than the East Coast," said Celine's mother. "A humid heat is so much more oppressive."

Native animals lived by their quickness. Doves and quail fluttered. Desert rats and squirrels scrabbled and bit. Jack and cottontail rabbits quivered. They ran in their heads even while standing still to chew a cactus pad. It appeared to Celine that most of these animals met their end in her backyard, ripped apart by cats, or coyotes, or hawks. With horrible frequency, she found little entrails full of half-digested green and decapitated heads nestled beneath the pine tree next to the pool.

"Don't be sad," her mother counseled. "It's just part of the natural cycle."

Once when Celine cornered a horned toad against a stone wall, it shot blood from its eyes. The strange streaks remained on her T-shirt, even after washes.

"It's just that creature's defense mechanism," her mother explained.

Celine's mother was a priestess who practiced rituals of creams and ointments and aloe leaves split open so that the jelly innards could be rubbed over burns, cuts, and scratches.

Celine felt the desert was a science fiction. This landscape didn't appear in the real world or on TV except as the setting for alien planets and Westerns.

"Be sure to put on more sunscreen," reminded her mother as the sun burned and burned.

2.

Celine's father had been born in the same place and in the same year as the atomic bomb. Her grandfather had been a member of the military industrial complex. The Cold War arms race paid for her father's braces and family ski vacations. The underlying angst of annihilation was not discussed over cheerful dinners. For residents of her father's hometown the mushroom cloud was not an emblem of destruction but of great intellectual and technological achievement.

Celine's mother, when she was young, arrived to the desert as a freshman on scholarship from back east. She'd grown up with nuns at school and first generation white-collar Irish at home. Her universe was a track home with rose bushes and pastel appliances, school uniforms, and parental rage that fizzed up after the inevitable one-too-many Old Fashioneds. At eighteen her mother left steel-mill drab for turquoise fantasy.

The desert offered Celine's mother an emotional blank slate. It was for her an overexposed sandy stage on which to act out Zane Grey purple-sage passion plays accompanied by soundtracks of Dylan and Ronstadt and Hendrix. Catholicism fell away under the influence of dorm-room peyote. She made ceramics and studied womyns history.

In the beginning of their relationship, Celine's parents traveled up north and down to Mexico.

They camped in high and low deserts, in different kinds of western forests. Drank Tecates beneath pinions and various pines. Ate thumbnail-sized wild strawberries that grew beside Indian paintbrush and columbine. They traced paths around yucca and clumps of threadgrass, chaparral, and barrel cactus. The altitude let them see a distant hawk. They climbed hills and saw coyotes, a burrowing owl, and some white-tailed deer. Sometimes they caught sight of the border fence in the distance, at some points just a wire-thin line beside a dirt road. They passed their water bottle back and forth, and the hazy space of the Americas blurred.

Once they had Celine they bought a house on the outskirts. Homes in that neighborhood were containers for obscure Baby Boom dreams. Snowbirds with an extra-large RV and a gun case in the den lived across from the engineer and his dental hygienist wife. Bumpers stickered with Jesus fish and "In case of the rapture, this car will be unmanned." Down the road a pair of French university professors had a tennis court they played on daily. Across from them a pack of dogs ran laps inside a chain-link square. Further down, hippie retirees hung handmade flags above their geodesic dome.

At the end of the block was the empty, half-burned house. On the night of the fire that took that house, the children had been away at a sleepover. The family dog saved the mother but not the father. Robert Fountain died of smoke inhalation. Loretta Fountain moved to Dallas with the insurance money and grief, the neighbors said. No one bought the property though, so the house sat with a black hole where the roof had been and an empty pool out back.

Despite that property-devaluing mark of this tragedy, the neighborhood was solid middle class. Celine's mother said toto her father more than once over granola, which meant it was true.

3.

While other mothers wore their hair sprayed and their sweaters twinned, Celine's mother cultivated the style of a character from an Altman film: long straight hair, loose denim shirts, heavy turquoise bracelets. She smelled like lavender oil, black tea, and smoke. She navigated feminist waves of thought and taught her daughter it was not just right, but necessary to do the same.

She held the romantic ideals of the 1960s. She held these ideas in the 1980s when hippie revolution was neither style nor anti-style. As a mother she spoke of revolutions in education, of each child as a special flower or a light beneath a bushel basket. A flowery light. She preached the gospel of Summerhill. She aligned children and mothers with all the vulnerable people who struggled on the underside of history. She spoke about all this in PTA meetings in the fish-stick-smelling cafeteria of Celine's school. Heady parents and teachers nodded while others looked at the ceiling and thought perhaps the local university was to blame for this kind of talk. Theory, they sighed.

Even when she was too old for it, her mother read books aloud. It was because Celine was dyslexic, or as her teacher called her, lazy. Celine's mother fought for her daughter like she herself hadn't been fought for as a child.

The books were classic girl fictions: *Alice in Wonderland* and *Anne of Green Gables* and *Emily of New Moon* and all the *Little*

House books and *Jane Eyre* and *Wuthering Heights*. As if she had been there, Celine's mother spoke about prairie fires and scarlet fevers, initiation rituals and torrential downpours, family betrayals and corset-induced fainting spells. Her voice moved like a wagon. It moved like feet in leather moccasins padding through dust and starvation. Her voice lost children to fever. As her voice moved she stroked her braid with her free hand. Her knuckles like drought ground.

"Death is not getting to tell your story," her mother said. Her mother said the women she described were famous, but when Celine mentioned them to kids at school they didn't know who she was talking about.

"Women's role in history is repressed," her mother explained. "But don't let them worry you. Remember all stories are about survival," said her mother.

4.

Celine first met Julie at the auditions for the holiday production of *Peter Pan*. Celine had been in children's classes so she acted like an expert. Julie had just showed up because she was bored.

Julie was cast as the Lost Boy Nibs, while Celine got to be Unnamed Lost Boy #3. They were members of a gaggle of kids cast to populate Neverland scenes with motion and war whoops.

From the outside, the theater's architecture was so banal it might as well have been the DMV. But despite exterior modesty the interior was a series of enchanting spaces the girls came to adore over the course of rehearsals.

In the lobby mid-afternoon sun measured diagonal stripes through the blinds. Black velvet curtains hung inside the theater. Small rooms for dressing, for makeup, for construction, and for waiting hid behind and within.

In addition to the acting, the girls both started volunteering in the costume shop. They were given four hundred roses to sew onto the hem of Mrs. Darling's dress. They were the youngest in the shop so they got to quietly observe the grown-ups who had real parts.

The main characters—Peter and the Darling children—got to fly on a harnessed pulley system, but the Lost Boys had to pretend to fly by running. Celine and Julie agreed pretending to fly was corny, but the director told them to pretend it was thrilling, so they did.

During the run Celine and Julie watched Peter and Wendy, Tiger Lily, and Mrs. Darling change in the big shared women's dressing room. They watched some form of their future bodies take off street clothes and change into fantastical costumes. They watched these magical transformations. They tried not to annoy Donna Beth, watching only for a moment at a time as she bound her breasts before pulling on her tunic of fabric leaves. They wondered if they would become like these women when they got older.

They thought Donna Beth, who was playing Peter, was the coolest. She had a skateboarder haircut shaved up the back and a heavy smoking habit.

Celine and Julie wavered between believing in the beauty of the play and believing in the adults who were making the play through labor and artifice.

Because she was getting bored with kid stuff, Celine found

another play by Christopher Durang in which one character describes a production of *Peter Pan* falling apart. Durang's Peter asks the audience to clap for Tinkerbell, just like in the original Peter. The audience claps until their hands hurt, but the actress doesn't believe it's enough. In the play the actress breaks with the script to berate the audience. She yells, telling them they'd failed.

"Oh my gosh, I wish Donna Beth would do that."

"Can you imagine?"

"Too good."

Too many times goofing around bored, Celine would turn to Julie or Julie to Celine to say their favorite joke. Repetition made it funnier.

"You didn't clap hard enough," one would start.

"Now Tinkerbell is dead," the other would finish. It drove other kids in the play, the cooler ones, a little crazy.

One time the bitchy girl playing Tiger Lily glared and gestured towards the stage. Shut. Up. She mouthed.

Shut. Up. Celine and Julie mouthed to one another. Tiger Lily flipped them off and they imitated her. It escalated with gestures and mouthed insults until Tiger Lily almost missed her cue. The stage manager scolded them all post-show. She stressed the importance of seriousness. Tiger Lily glared death at them. Celine and Julie never felt quite like the right kind of theater girls.

5.

Julie's parents had been Seattle hippies. Evidence of this included photographs of Julie's mother, young and smiling in homemade dresses next to her young father, standing jaunty next to the pile of wood he'd split. Her parents loved recounting epic be-ins, anti-logger protests, and voyages in their green Dodge Caravan with a mattress in back.

Julie was born in a bathtub in a wooden house. From there her parents took their water baby beach camping, on ferry rides to Anacortes, on hikes along Wildside Trail.

A wholesome love of adventure ran in the family. A baby picture hung in the hall, of Julie strapped to her grandfather's back as he posed before a mountain vista. There was another photo of Julie in an embroidered shirt from their trip to Oaxaca. There were many photos of her riding along rivers and trails on the shoulders of smiling men who her father hung out with—shaggy, early eighties burnouts and nice, countercultural science nerds.

She did not remember the scenes she saw in the photos, but she did remember the brown floral sheets in the wooden house's guest room. She remembered red ants fleeing in sticky confusion after she squirted her juice box down their hole. She remembered her father's friends laughing around a bonfire in the backyard long past bedtime. She remembered strawberries in rows in the garden and a metal Muppets lunchbox beside a plastic Rainbow Brite lunchbox. She remembered crying over math problems as her dad tried to explain. She remembered shoelace tying and cat chasing. She remembered ballet classes in a big, old studio with windows on two sides. Through the windows on nice days she smelled yeast from a brewery.

She remembered the Washington years as a series of cool, wet bursts of air through open windows.

When Julie was ten her dad got a job at the university in the southwestern town. The first time she heard about Las Cruces she burst into tears, but the move had already been set in motion.

Her mother drove their Subaru with Julie, their two cats Brownie and Mr. Bill, and a bunch of houseplants, while her father drove a U-Haul with the rest of their stuff. They left the cool lands of childhood to the heat of a new life. Along the long way her mother alternated between NPR and her favorite tapes. Bob Edwards and Bonnie Raitt. Terry Gross and Willie Nelson. The most constant throughline was Paul Simon. *Graceland.* The road-trip album was both lullaby and the early morning soundtrack. Julie and her mom memorized lyrics. They would be able to sing along with *Graceland* for the rest of their lives. They stayed in multiple Days Inns. Julie read the *Little House* books up to *By The Shores of Silver Lake.* She barely saw Death Valley, even though her mother pestered her to take in the mystical landscape, because who knew if or when she'd be there again.

6.

Julie and Celine huddled in hoodies and blankets draped around their shoulders. It was one of the nights Donna Beth babysat while Julie's parents attended a cultural center fundraiser. The girls were allowed to have a fire in the backyard.

"Don't burn the house down," half-joked her father.

They had cigarettes. They had vodka siphoned into water bottles. Julie replaced what they'd taken by watering down the bottle in her parents' cabinet. The perfect crime. Julie sang restless lyrics. She rolled her eyes at Celine and danced half into the dark. She ducked and drank, prompting Celine to imitate. The flavorless mouthfuls burned and Celine pulled up · her knees to make herself as small as possible on the patio chair.

Smoke curled around them. Donna Beth called from offstage. They made nervous faces and Celine hid her bottle while Julie downed hers.

"What are you doing out here?" They were doing nothing. Donna Beth took pity on them. In a bored big-sister way she was mean-nice, or nice-mean. She said she would read them a horror story from a birthday gift book.

"Billy Jackson told townspeople that a black dog followed him wherever he went, but no one ever saw it. When they saw him on the road hollering they thought he'd gone crazy.

"He first saw the dog the day he shot Jesse Major. There wasn't much law enforcement, so Billy was never charged. People thought it shameful, but there wasn't much to be done.

"The Majors and Jacksons had been feuding since the land was Indian Territory. The day Billy met Jesse, Jesse drew first, but Billy fired quicker. Jesse tumbled. Jesse pleaded for his life, but Billy still killed him. It was when he lay dying that the black dog ran up. It whimpered and licked the boy's face. It barked at Billy.

"Get," he screamed and in his fear he shot the bitch as he had her master.

"The night after, Billy woke to a scratching at the door. My mind goes wild, he thought, pulling the blanket close. The next day he neither saw nor heard anything strange. But the next night he was woken by an animal noise at the door.

"'Let that bitch try and come,' he growled, this time holding his gun.

"From then on, when Billy walked through the woods he thought he glimpsed the dog following at a distance. He was woken nights by sounds that he told himself were the wind. But in the mornings the yard always had a musty stink. To neighbors he told of black hairs on the floor and sofa, on his pillow even. He would pick something from his jacket and hold it before their eyes. They remarked to one another, 'This country can destroy a man's mind.'

"Things went like this until neighbors took his madness as normal. Then one winter someone noticed there was no smoke rising from Billy's chimney. He was nowhere. So they searched around till he was found, body on the frozen ground. At first they thought somebody had killed him. He had enemies to be sure, but they found no marks of violence on his body. He was still young and the community found his death strange, but there was nothing to be done.

"It was said that the coroner found a great many black hairs all about Billy's clothes and body and even his face. Those who attended his funeral said that even washed and laid out in Sunday best, his body still gave off a strong and unmistakable scent of dog."

From the dark surrounding the girls came a few barks, then a sustained howl. More barks and growls, this time closer. The girls started screaming, for the pleasure of screaming and partly because they were scared. Out of the dark a man rushed, grabbing Donna Beth, who was already caught in laughing-shrieking.

"Run away, children," Donna Beth's boyfriend said. "I'm a monster come to eat this girl up."

7.

As was habit, Celine's grandparents came down from the north for the holiday. On Christmas Eve, Celine and her grandmother took on the task of putting out the luminarias, or as they were controversially called in the north, farolitos. The desert tradition was to put out these lights so the spirit of baby Jesus could find his way.

It was a little cool. Celine wore her puffy jacket and her grandmother wore a sensible windbreaker and pearl earrings. They went along the driveway placing a paper lunch bag with sand and a tea light at even intervals. Then lit the candles with long-nozzled safety lighters.

"What did you learn this fall?" asked her grandmother. Celine didn't reply.

Once it was fully dark Celine sat in the back seat next to her mother and grandmother as her grandfather chatted about politics with her father. They drove slow though residential lanes and around cul-de-sacs to see all the decorations, admiring the subtle details and making fun of the crass displays. Luminaria made darkened homes into simple shapes. Little smudgy gold dots of light made squares and rectangles in an undifferentiated dry dark. A few houses later, strings of electric-blue icicles festooned porches and plastic Santas and reindeer froze on rooftops.

They ended up in the plaza. Old-town businesses had overwhelmed the church square with thousands of lights. Her grandfather bought a round of hot apple cider. They drove home for another ritual cycle of sleep and waking.

The day after the day, on December 26th, her grandparents suggested a visit across the border to the craft market and a family dinner at their favorite Mexican restaurant.

They drove beside a stretch of new subdivision homes, an outlet store mall, and highway chain motels made to look like some kind of alpine chalet. Celine's mother sighed, "Things were so different when I first arrived. The area still had its own flavor."

"What the region needs is jobs," her grandfather countered. Conversation lapsed.

The water made a clear sound as it hit the multicolored tiles of the courtyard fountain. The waitress placed down a white oval plate with a center of enchiladas, chicken mole, and for Celine's father, a combination special wreathed in rice and beans and the symbolic vegetable gesture of iceberg confetti and tomato bits. The adults spoke of Colorado, water rights, and local officials. Celine ripped her white flour tortilla and let the red chili soak through.

As mariachi "Silent Night" played through the speakers, the waitress cleared the table, then offered Kahlua over ice cream. The adults said yes—it was a holiday after all.

Parrots in their wrought-iron cage screamed as Celine found a last alcoholic smudge on her spoon. She felt a riot she could neither spell nor speak. Beside the green birds, piranhas circled in the murky light of their narrow tank.

Driving back across the border, they could not see, but sensed all the houses hiding without electricity. The too-many churches glowed orange. Cedar smoke and diesel exhaust blew through vents. Fire in the desert was always a distress signal because it was all so dry. Celine saw bonfires.

"What are those?"

"For pilgrims," her mother said.

"They crawl on hands and knees. Some even self-flagellate with barbed whips."

As her mother and father criticized those religious devotees, Celine filled in the unknown with *National Geographic* memory images of blood on the white shirts of men sweating

24

in a town square. The men held short whips before others who shouldered a cross. Bright sun made the blood gloss. She thought about when her former best friend fell on a barrel cactus. Her T-shirt with a pony was pinned to chest flesh and in the dozens of places, blood made polka dots. Her friend's screams went on and on that afternoon.

"I read in the *Sun* that the climb is more dangerous now because people have started hiding in the mountains and robbing the pilgrims. It is not even that they have much besides jewelry or beepers." Her father coughed. "People can be such idiots."

Her mother shook her head and then they all went silent as the car twisted along until the fires disappeared behind another hill.

8.

Celine never said "Daddy" and she squirmed when other girls did. As a child she refused to sit on her father's lap. Their hugs were tense. Around her seventh birthday her father had begun traveling for work and his already distant presence faded further. At twelve, she told her mom, "I don't think I love him." Her mother replied, "You don't mean that."

Though they were uncomfortable talking, Celine and her father both liked late-night TV. While he stretched on the couch, she perched at a catlike distance in an armchair.

The ritual bound them. Same ten o'clock, same anchors—Patricia Castillo with glossy hair and Robert Harmon with a voice as even as the dishwasher—same couch of pastel Aztec print, same father in a succession of rumpled oxfords. A Friday; a Tuesday; a house fire; an election; a shooting; a council meeting; a ceremony at Fort Bliss; a maquiladora opening; road closings; a drunk-driving accident on I-95. Remember to change your clocks forward an hour, remember to change them back. Images reflected off the night living room window half-hidden behind the curtains. Sometimes wind blew the mesquite bushes' branches against the glass, other times the ballpark kliegs beamed. After the hard stuff, the anchors rounded towards sports and weather. The Diablos won their home game. Odd-numbered houses can water their lawns tomorrow. The high will be 95. The high will be 100. The TV producers knew repetition made comfort; content barely mattered.

Her father got up for a last glass of water, turned off the lights and locked the back door, switched stations to *The Tonight Show*. One of their cats turned around and around to form his sleep circle. Celine retreated to the bathroom to study her thin arms in the wall mirror, rubbing her mother's anti-wrinkle cream into her baby face.

"A light protects me," she told herself.

This was the spell she repeated into sleep under her quilt. Above her the window reflected the night. Her white wall, half-lit, was just a smudge in the destroying dark. Outside, the desert stretched out and out for hundreds of miles in all directions.

9.

The stage filled with actors warming up.

They paced and stretched their arms while repeating words with exaggerating lips.

The actors repeated, "An annoying noise annoys an oyster."

They repeated, "The sixth sick sheik's sixth sheep's sick" and "six thick thistle sticks." They repeated, "What gall to play ball in this small hall . . . around the rough and rugged rock." They paced the stage sing-songing "the ragged rascal ran" and "red leather, yellow leather." All this they repeated to warm "the teeth, the cheeks, the tip of the tongue."

"Half-hour," the stage manager called. She wove between stage and makeup room, lighting booth and wings, a woman in baggy black sweatshirt with a stopwatch around her neck like a disapproving coach.

The actors retreated to their dressing rooms to change, dropping Levis on chair backs and trading white undershirts and leopard-print bras for linen undershirts and boned corsets. Suck in and pull. Touch and gaze. Into the mirror, eyes gazing at themselves as they applied powder, fake blood, moles, wigs, perfect lips—makeup as the designer had taught them. Through the speakers came unobtrusive mood-setting music, the sound of spectators entering, seats creaking.

"Doors," warned the manager.

"Places, please," said the stage manager. In the wings the crew made silent jokes, pantomimed blow jobs and pratfalls. Stagehand boys whispered, "Donna Beth, you look hot."

The lights fell and everyone went silent. Then all at once those assembled plunged into some parallel reality.

"I pray thee, Rosalind, sweet my coz, be merry," Donna Beth said, making her first entrance as Shakespeare's Celia.

The performance lapped in sweaty waves of agony and ecstasy. Fights were feigned, memorized speeches were lost then found. Pulling off that dramatic rise before the intermission made up for a mess of a scene. The audience was an abstract, viscose mass, sometimes laughing. You couldn't hear if they cried, but it was palpable when it occurred. Applause. The end.

After the play, cast and crew emerged from the theater. Night air cooled skin burning with adrenaline. No one except the grown-ups was tired. But even the grown-ups weren't grown-ups. They wanted to hang out.

At after-parties Celine and Julie got to see how the women flirted with each other and the boys. For a while everyone appeared like smarter, funnier, more attractive versions of themselves. The actors' personalities blurred with the characters they'd just finished playing.

For the first time they saw houses surrounded with dead grass and stocked with liquor. Houses belonging to adults who were not parents. This is when the girls first learned why theater was made in the dark.

Because it was a special occasion Julie's parents said they could be out until midnight. Teachers from the university were there. It was supposed to be all proper, but because of the smallness of the town and the largeness of the desert, ages mixed inappropriately. The night unraveled.

Celine and Julie felt sophisticated even with just ginger ale. At some point in the evening some random person would slip them a bit of rum or something.

"Don't tell."

The thickset, soon-to-be-divorced movement teacher kept whispering to his favorite girl student, who was small and blonde and newly lesbian. He was magically free, post-show, since his wife didn't like parties. The recently divorced director from New York said she could let her hair down because it was a Friday. She opened wine from her "little collection." The guy that prayed in the bathroom before shows crushed a case of beer on his own. The gay boy got handsy with the ingénue, holding her from behind and joking that she was like Janet Jackson. She shrieked and slapped his arm before they collapsed in hugs declaring their love for one another. The older guy who'd dropped out and then returned to study lighting design kept going out to smoke and returning to the kitchen with glazed eyes. The freshman described his high school at the reservation up north. The singer from out of state held a beer bottle in her cleavage as a joke, which got the Texas boy worked up. He kept telling her to "do it again." She laughed but pulled a jean jacket over her tank top. Comfort was a state with blurry borders.

Julie, buzzy, rolled her eyes at Celine.

"We'd better go before they all have an orgy."

"Don't be ridiculous, we can stay a little longer."

10.

Celine's driveway was a sand horseshoe around a center thicket of mesquite, creosote ephedra, and beavertail. Celine sat in Julie's idling car until the end of "Come as You Are," staring into spiny overlap of branches visible in headlight beams.

"Why are you crying?"

"I don't even know."

Celine felt the pattern of branches inside her as a state of tangled sensations, scratched dull surfaces wrapping tough wood. Do these bushes even have sap? She sopped and snotted inside while waiting for the flicker of recognition that would bridge her pain and Julie's seeming calm. What she desired most was recognition. As if onstage, she unhooked her seatbelt and opened the door, all quick and slow motion.

"Call me tomorrow."

She walked the little way from car to gate, turning in the glare of headlight to wave, signaling I'm safe, goodbye.

She moved from outdoor set to the interior's glow. In her own familiar kitchen, she felt more fucked-up high than she had at Julie's. The brown tiles grew while the distance between the counters shrank. It smelled of her mother's uninspired soup of carrots, onions, rice, and beans. She shaved off a sliver of the cornbread still out from dinner. Her father had the news on in the living room.

The repetition of the news made for comfort; the content didn't matter. Same couch of pastel Aztec print, same father, same time, same combination of old man and young woman onscreen. Images reflected off the black living room window half-hidden behind the curtains as an anchor said, "Eighteen-year-old Sabrina Martinez left her Juárez home at about 3 p.m. last Tuesday to meet a friend. She has not been seen since. The police are seeking further information."

Celine heard her father sigh heavy, then flip the channel. She walked the gauntlet between him and the TV towards the safety of the bathroom.

"Goodnight," he called.

"Mumhum."

In the bathroom she studied the freckles on her nose before spreading anti-wrinkle cream beneath her eyes.

"This is what being drunk feels like. But you won't die," she told her mirror-self. Words were not in the visceral chaos.

Curled in a fetal ball in bed she kept up a whispered repetition, "Don't be scared, don't be scared."

She dreamed she was awake in bed all night, in the black box of the ranch home fading into the too much darkness of the desert.

Julie's father was the dean of engineering and her mother knew how to host events that called for hors d'oeuvres. The haphazard hippie style of their youth had evolved into upmarket folk art decoration, and a nice stereo system with all their favorite records repurchased in CD form. Her dad and mom strategized his move into administration for a higher salary. They talked about her grandparents' assisted living bills.

Her mom hung two large red and black paintings in the sunken living room. Two Navajo blankets hung over two rawhide sidechairs that no one ever sat in. The chairs flanked a Spanish colonial-style shelf repurposed as a liquor cabinet. Julie was forbidden from wearing shoes in the house and had to police friends who came over. The house was kept magazine-clean with the help of a housekeeper named Yolanda. Julie's mother's tips were conscientiously liberal. Julie's parents, unlike Celine's, were public beings active within the city and university ecologies.

The picture window framed the mountain range named after a conquistador. The girls sat side by side on the leather couch. Someone walking by outside would have seen them framed by the window in the act of drinking tequila snuck from the liquor cabinet. From the sidewalk the girls would have appeared like actors on screen film. The sunset reflected against the window in bands of reds, pinks, blacks, and blues.

"Guess what I got."

"What?"

"Pot!"

"Oh my goshhh . . . Where'd you get it?"

"Miguel."

They exchanged wide-eyed silent reactions.

"We have to go outside though."

The air smelled like fall, like chilis roasting in drums. Celine nervously pinched when Julie passed the burning joint. Their two heads, one curly red, the other dark and glossy straight, came close together while they smoked.

The scent of pot gave Celine a flash when she realized she'd smelled it many times before. It had been there all this time in the folds of her mom's clothes. She'd found it when her mom had hugged her.

Smelling it, getting high, felt like walking through a door she'd seen but never been able to find the handle for.

Even though Julie knew her parents were gone for the night, she still got nervous whenever cars passed.

"I want to tell you something."

"Anything." Celine looked so serious.

"You know how my mom seems sad a lot?"

"I guess."

"She is. Really sad. It's because of my cousin Amber. She used to live with my grandparents. For my mother I think she was like a younger sister, because my aunt sort of dropped out as a mom.

"When I was eleven Amber came to visit us here. She was on her way to a volunteer program in Mexico with her boyfriend. She was like a beautiful hippie or something, and he was like a handsome rock star. I mean that's stupid, but that was how they looked to me.

"I remember my parents were so worried, but at the same time so proud because they said she was doing interesting things with her life. Following her destiny or whatever. I was jealous. So they went and we got lots of colorful postcards for a while.

"Then in the winter, one day I came home from school and both my parents were home, and they said Amber had died. Her kidney failed when she was in a tiny town without a hospital."

Julie did not know what to say. The high silence and the intensity of Celine's face made things change size. Their space moved out, becoming vast and similar, similar to what she could not say.

"My grandparents had been all worried before, about kidnapping, about violence or something, and my parents, even though they were worried too, they would just say 'she'll be fine. She's brave and she's with someone who loves her.' But then, I feel like it broke something for my mom when she died.

"It's been two years. I hear my mom like, sobbing about it on the phone all the time still. There's something so wrong."

12.

The most famous theater person in their town was a silver-haired playwright/director who'd won a Tony in the 1970s and an Oscar in the '80s.

His male characters were tortured and whip-sharp. His female characters were few and feral. The playwright was habitually criticized for his reductive and salacious sexual scenes and his glorification of violence. In one of his plays a woman bites off a man's tongue and his mouth becomes a blossoming wound. This happened onstage and always created a headache for the makeup designers who would have to make many careful little packets of fake blood. The girls had heard that two other plays featured rapes of toxic slut characters. His plays were in the Sam Shepard universe in their preoccupation with the West and in their dealings with adult themes that were inappropriate for young viewers. At least that's what Celine and Julie's parents thought.

Though Donna Beth had appeared in two of his plays, Celine and Julie had not been allowed to attend. But now that they were older their parents thought they could handle it. It was a new work.

They heard some gossip at the theater that this current work was inspired by Donna Beth. There were some suspicions that the writer and actress might have, at some point, crossed the line, despite his marriage and their age difference. The women at the costume shop shot each other significant looks.

On the night of the performance the girls sat in the dark theater, dressed up in department store velvet. Subtext swirled.

Donna Beth was a Lolita-type character who wandered onstage periodically when the curtain was closed to give knowing monologues about violence.

Besides Donna Beth's character, there was a teacher character she was having an affair with, a boyfriend character, and a stepfather character. There were no other women in the play except for her mother, who appeared only as a pair of legs sticking out from a doorway in the final scene.

A lot of the play was above the girls' heads. They forgot most of it, except for Donna Beth's last big speech. She appeared in a spotlight made up in sleep-smeared shadow and rouge. Her features were blurry. She smoked a cigarette in the rehearsed manner of a girl acting natural.

Though Donna Beth's character was a little thin, people thought her acting gave the play a power beyond itself. She paced and whispered magnetically. She broke the fourth wall. She smirked at the audience a little, flirting.

"I don't like thinking about high school. I try not to remember, and what I remember I try not to care about. My mother couldn't afford to see life beyond next month. I found it depressing. It was my grandparents who paid for ballet classes and my car. They liked to punish her by spoiling me. I got a state scholarship that paid for college, but only in-state. I chose the local college because my grandparents promised a car. New Mexico is called 'the land of enchantment,' but my friends and I prefer 'the land of entrapment.' I took this history of film class my first year. The teacher was this weird old guy. God knows how he ended up with us in this dead desert town. But he showed us so many good films. I learned who I was by watching these beautiful film women.

"I think it was the first day, he showed us a film of the first recorded death. The electrocution of Topsy the elephant. It got me. A moment before the electricity flows the animal appears calm, as if waiting. Then, a billow of white smoke. White smoke around a gray elephant in a black-and-white silent film. Her death is silent. It takes only twenty-three seconds.

"I met my boyfriend that first semester, too. He got me into the theater. When we were falling in love he taught me this trick. Try it," she instructed. "Turn to the person next to you and do this with me. Look into one another's eyes and mouth the words 'elephant shoes.' Do it again and watch their lips. It looks like you are saying 'I love you.' Do it again. Do it until you feel something."

Donna Beth had tears streaming down her face. The audience—the chubby, provincial locals who were unaccustomed to crying—were crying too. She was performing something they didn't know they needed until they saw her doing it. She said it again and again, elephant shoes, elephant shoes. She kept saying it with a falling voice, quieter and quieter, until she was mouthing the words. Celine and Julie never forgot this.

At just the right moment the stage went black. If these people had had roses, they would have thrown them.

The girls wanted more than anything to be just like her.

13.

Miguel. Julie only let herself look halfway up his forearm to where his tattoo began. The air through his window slapped her.

Miguel. He had a slow voice but a funny way when he'd tease with a sidelong glance. He turned onto a dirt road parallel to the highway that dead-ended at concrete drainage tunnels. The lights went in but didn't make it out the other side. They parked on a hill where they could watch the sun set in the valley. Her nerves ached, aware with what it meant to be in a parked car with a boy. He didn't touch her but instead leaned his head back and told her this story while she focused on the dinged white paint of the glove compartment.

"When I was a teenager I lived for a year with my mother. Our shitty apartment had a view of the port, so I'd spend my time when she was at work getting high and watching the ships.

"I hated everyone except this one girl Larissa. It wasn't romantic between us, but I was maybe a little bit in love, or lust. Anyway the days I skipped, she would call at night to tell me what I'd missed. I could have given a fuck. But I liked her voice in the dark, narrating the just-past. How Mr. Gutierrez lost his shit; blah blah blah . . . How all Suzanna talked about at lunch was the Selena concert she went to.

"So this one night I decided I would confide in her a private feeling. I was in my dark bedroom. I tried to tell her about the feeling I got listening to her with my eyes in the dark. It's as if the room is stretching out far beyond the walls. I feel this shape-shifting, until the room becomes vast in my confused senses. Spreading out and out."

"What did she say?"

"Real matter-of-fact she said, 'Oh yes, there's a name for that phenomenon. It's normal. Everyone feels that.'"

Whether or not Miguel was best for the role, there had to be *the boy, the man* for Julie. She was going to find one, so he became that one. Whether or not it made sense, some boy was going to touch Julie. The part was there as a negative space. She was on the lookout. His body fit the space. His voice filled her head. She found him fascinating and made him tell her all his stories.

He told the myth of his family like a flat but colorful film. His mother was from Colombia, though she'd moved to Miami in the '70s. His mother married his father to stay in the States, partly, but she had also been in love with the man for better or—as it ended up—for worse. They'd divorced when he was just three, so as far as memory was concerned they'd always been apart. His father was a white guy raised in Florida who'd adopted New Mexico as a home. He was a former Marine who taught at Transmountain Community College. He'd married and divorced again after Miguel's mom, so he didn't bother anymore. He'd moved west because it was easy. He had drinking buddies and camping buddies because there were a lot of military men in the area. He dated some women. Whatever. Miguel followed him here for some tuition break, but he didn't like his dad much though, so.

When he met Julie she didn't tell him her age, and how was he supposed to have guessed given she was always at the theater where everyone else was college age or a full-on adult. Julie wanted him in her play and what did he care? She was cute enough and her trip was none of his business.

Since high school Miguel had sold pot and other stuff on occasion, just to cover basics. He drove a white VW Bug, a car almost no one had in the States anymore, but that was still quite popular over the border. High school had been a haze, but he'd been getting serious since moving. His plan was to become an English teacher like his father but, he hoped, without the crippling alcoholism that caused his father to hide bottles in the toilet tank and the toolbox. He told Miguel his drinking was under control, don't doubt.

14.

It was easy in the afternoon. Miguel suggested they go over the border. He mentioned it like it was nothing.

"After," he said, "we can stop by my cousin's and say hi."

On the US side everyone drove, but in Juárez it felt like life was lived on the streets.

On the other side of the border, rust-colored stucco and melon-hued interior walls made faces more luminous. There were long open alleys lined on both sides with stalls filled with leather belts, cobalt and canary glazed plates, decorative swords, sombreros, paired señorita and señor puppets. Tourist stuff.

Men said "hello, please come in" outside craft stalls in a bored and easy way, because they repeated it all day at the wandering Texas shoppers. "Come in, come in. Yes, it's good quality and good prices." Chubby ladies in too-tight jeans and pastel T-shirts dragged toddlers. A group of men gathered around the open door of a Dodge Ram blasting KISS FM. Miguel laughed at Julie when she couldn't stop gripping his arm and saying, "Look, that's so pretty" as she pointed out a couple retreating behind an amber-painted door, or a bougainvillea growing straggly out of a cobalt-tiled planter. This was how things were supposed to look, Julie told him, like the films she'd seen set in some charged otherworldly world.

They got tacos. At each plastic-covered picnic table beneath a Corona umbrella people ate carne, onion, and cilantro-filled tacos accompanied by agua fresca ladled from huge glass jars. The sun diffused through the watermelon water, the white horchata, the pulpy limeade. Steam added a layer, making the juices play with the light like stained glass. A grandmotherly woman in a white lace blouse made coffee. That Selena song played for the millionth time on the radio. Julie watched a mother spoon ice cream into her baby's mouth.

Across the street, a whole band in matching outfits emerged from a van. Miguel bought another beer. The surroundings stirred a desire for this and other elsewheres. Julie squeezed Miguel's hand beneath the table.

15.

After her mother went to bed to read, always so early, Celine would watch the beginning of *Law & Order* with her father. Sometimes she watched the whole show and sometimes just the set-up. The crimes were always outlined in the first five minutes. Some young woman raped, some rich man bludgeoned. The plot lines were taken from real-life crimes. Ripped from the headlines, they said.

Some of the storylines disturbed her, but she always liked the grimy city setting. New York was for her a real fantasy, like palm-treed LA or some distant place called Europe.

Law & Order provided another comforting rhythm in the week. Each Thursday night at 9 p.m., a new brutal attack was followed by a swift rotation of justice. It was all so fictional.

On nights when the premise of the episode seemed boring or too scary, she would run a bath and slip behind the blue-flowered shower curtain into the intimate realm of steam-sweaty tiles and diffused light. The *dum-dum* of the after-commercial theme music would drift in periodically from the living room.

Looking down on her body created a distorted view. Standing in the mirror she conceived of herself as thin, but lying down, her new soft parts fell to the side: breasts and hip flesh. All the words came backwards and shameful.

"Ugg," she whispered. "Fat bitch."

When she was younger she sometimes put her hand under the tap and ran the water hot without cold. The burning was so intense it felt freezing. Her eyes traveled down from her slippery breasts to her stomach, a stomach in no way washboard, then down to her hips, which looked loose and all too grabbable. She measured a span with thumb and first finger. The place she chose was below hipbone.

The first time that she drew the razor she'd been too timid. So the second time she pressed down hard. The fresh blade cut deeper than anticipated. But what's to be called anticipated when cutting yourself open? On later nights she figured out by feel how hard to press. She threw away each blade after cutting to remain pure. She'd bought a whole box of them at Walgreens. Afterwards, she washed each cut with hydrogen peroxide.

She never again experienced a cut as clean as the first. Her skin opened to reveal a miniature valley. She saw inside a white cliff of fat. Her eye went into the space faster than the pain could. Her living flesh paused the length of a heartbeat before the blood flooded in. It was an exquisite instant. The space between perceiving and feeling pain stretched her time, though not long enough. The water browned with diffused throb as the blood emerged. She wept with shock and relief, looking at her body as a raw material. At a remove she felt both self-pity and disgust. Her body ultra-real and dreamt. She made a toilet paper rose then dyed it red.

"Don't be scared," she repeated to the bathwater, the tiles, her shaking hands.

She heard the closing credit music of the show coming from the living room. She pulled the plug of the bath.

"Don't be scared," she said to her mother in the other room, and to the whole town she hated without articulable reason.

That first night, her terror was replaced with a comforting sensation of injury. Feeling hurt felt special.

"You are protected by a white light," she told herself before falling asleep in her south-facing room that had become a private hospital, cradling the throbbing pain that made that night vivid.

16.

Girls needed only say no to intoxicants, but if they decided they wanted them, substances would always appear. Celine and Julie learned this lesson. They began to say, "No, I know what I like."

There were Tecates, Buds, 40s in people's fridges. In cabinets there were bottles of Cuervo bought cheap at the last crossing to Mexico. On special occasions people made sweet drinks with mixers and cut-up fruits. Whiskey sours, agua de piñas, palomas. These were the kinds of drinks boys would make for girls to show they cared about what girls liked. Thoughtful like that.

Besides drinks there was always some boy around who had prescriptions obtained without prescription, pills squirreled away in a backpack pocket. Will you take it? Sure. Whatever.

For the high school girls, after school was more open than late nights. In that span of afternoon time no one's parents were wondering where they were. Celine and Julie could slip into the parallel realm, a free space of honey-slanted light, *Simpsons* reruns, and bong hits. The air was warm and dry when the whoever assembled flopped down on the broken plaid couch propped up on cinderblocks.

When Miguel had strangers over to his apartment the girls would say no, mostly. However when it was just the three of them, they would say yes. Something about his bedroom eyes, something about how he turned consuming into a lesson:

"Exhale slow, but don't worry, coughing is good too," he would say. It all made getting high a secret ritual of charged friendship. Celine and Julie would get all dumb mystical while Miguel laughed at them. The girls would say yes in those instances. In stoned times they would discuss how drugs were, like, gateways. They would say, "We're going into the secret space together."

One time, in relation to some half-joke, Miguel said they

should beg like dogs, and so they did. The girls crawled around on all fours, barking while Miguel watched bemused but also kind of turned on.

"Dirty bitches," he mumbled, all intense.

Celine got self-conscious and stopped. She went to the bathroom to wash her face and when she came back out Miguel and Julie were making out. It was time for Celine to go; her mom would stress if she wasn't there for dinner. Miguel rolled his eyes while Julie, sighing, agreed to drive her home.

17.

Like clubs the world over, the Day and Night sidestepped specifics of time and location in favor of laser lights and blunt-force bass. Though located in Mexico, it dealt mainly in American currency. It had one-dollar margaritas and three windowless floors. Technically Miguel got them in, but really the doormen were not in the habit of studying young girls' IDs too closely. It was their first time in a for-real club. Unnervingly easy to just walk in.

Knots of men tangled around the bar. Factory workers on date night; college kids blowing loan money; military boys from the base with fuzzy buzz cuts; older dudes of ambiguous status. The signifiers of class, nationality, and style affiliation mingled in hair gels and grease, colognes and strong soaps, crisp versus rumpled jeans, faded T-shirts versus polos versus oxfords in turquoise and pink. Cowboy boots versus broken Doc Martens versus Nike just out of the box versus Converse covered in duct tape. Tattooed forearms and shoulders and necks. The difference between freshman year and probation.

Dry humping, coke, and threats made an ambient drone below "Macarena" and "What is Love?" Boys' malleable definitions of safety and excess. Men's rules.

From out of the pounding dark, police appeared.

Miguel said they'd better go.

18.

They snuck back into Julie's living room but kept the lights off. In ditch-weed-induced hyper-boredom Celine and Julie watched movies late at night. Her parents had cable. They needed to practice escape before escaping. Something smashed against the window. Celine shrieked.

"How are we going to get out of here?" asked Celine.

"Here?"

"The desert. This whole place."

"The real question you need to ask yourself," said Julie, preparing her expression, "is are we not drawn onward to new era?"

"I don't get it."

"Are we no t draw n on ward to ne wera?"

"What are you even saying?"

"A-r-e w-e n-o-t d-r-a-w-n o-n-w-a-r-d t-o n-e-w e-r-a?"

"I-d-o-n-t-k-n-o-w-w-h-a-t-y-o-u-m-e-a-n."

"It's a spell." Julie laughed, "for you, my bad speller. Miguel taught it to me. It goes the same backward and forward."

To get closer to sleep they took Valium, which gave their film nights an extra dreamlike glaze.

Onscreen, a child muttered curse words at his father's funeral. Julie closed then opened her eyes. The widow mother remarried. The children wept. They formed a resistance to their mother's cruel new suitor. Flowers fell from the trees. How long was Celine asleep? The two children were taken away from the theater to their new home with sparse furnishings and Biblical pictures, rain and thunder. Their Swedish voices swam fishlike through the night living room.

"You have been living in an artificial world, entangled in artificial feelings. It is not my fault that reality is a hell," declared the cruel stepfather.

Amidst more rain a man paid a call to rescue the children from their stepfather. He used magic. Safe at the theater the children's uncle transformed into a puff of smoke. He was a real magician.

"We pass our lives in a wonderful self-deception," said the beautiful but sad widow, as if that were meant to explain the situation. The children were sent to bed, but later, the boy awoke, needing to pee. While looking for the toilet he found instead his father's ghost and heard God's voice behind a door. God was a giant puppet who may have in fact been the uncle magician. Celine pulled the pilled blue-green afghan closer. Why did sleep on the couch feel so much better than sleep in her bed?

Onscreen, family joy and a life of playful plays were restored. The children and their mother were again immersed in the world of art. Onstage, the uncle pretended to be dying, rehearsing. Finally the children's sweet mother said, "Meeting each other and leaving each other. Leaving and meeting. That's what life is!"

As Celine slept beside her, Julie cried half-asleep into a throw pillow.

Backstage pulleys creaked curtains into wings. The waves of black velvet disappeared only to reveal another curtain, a red one. From offstage came the sound of a scuffle, followed by someone shoving Donna Beth onstage. She was wearing a cocktail dress, strapless and too adult for her. Her eyes were glassy as if drugged.

"You know what kind of people kill each other most?" she asked the audience, pausing only slightly before answering her own question. "Family people."

Her speech was a patchwork of other speeches. It would have been clichéd if she had not been doing them so well.

"'All the world's a stage,' is a popular saying in our town, just like 'laugh now, cry later.' My old neighbors had it airbrushed on their pickup truck gate. It makes living sound like a game we're playing rather than traveling through.

"But that phrase, 'All the world's a stage,' comes from *As You Like It*, the play in which the most brilliant character is a woman pretending to be a man to protect herself in a wild environment.

"It's not her speech though. It belongs to this melancholic clown. He goes on about how through life, we—but he means men—mewl, puke, whine, like gross babies. Then as we grow, he says, we sigh like furnaces, because we are in love. I remember that part because I think of James's breath almost burning my neck in his car."

She paused to recall, wobbled in her high heels while she searches the dark for the next moment. The audience belonged to her.

"So what Shakespeare is telling us is that men have these different periods, and life progresses predictably from one to the other. Men fight, love, judge, and have children, before becoming old, and thus childlike again.

"And then they die."

She beamed like her good student alter ego.

"The important thing to realize—my director told me this—is that Shakespearean comedies and tragedies are often similar. But at the end of the tragedy all the disguises and complications lead to death, whereas in the comedies all the complications are, for the most part, unraveled so that order can be restored.

"All the world's a stage for theater brats. All the world's a stage for noble women disguising themselves as shepherds. All the world's a stage for those who want to perform transformation. They make stages to represent the stages they're going through. Like bad children."

Shifting her tone, she pouts for her audience.

"Are you bad like that?"

The moment lengthened and the room tensed. This aroused people, she could tell, because the seats squeaked beneath their asses. She'd turned them on. She laughed at them, knowing. Charge of electricity. Flicker of the follow spot.

"This is better than nothing, right? You're feeling good, aren't you? I want you to.

"People like stories, like characters they can relate to, or at least pity. They like Westerns with incest, or at least some kind of lurid sex and violence. People like pretty faces."

Turning onstage, she sighs.

"People don't like avant-garde shit.

"It's boring.

"Weird, inexplicable stuff is already happening in life, whereas art should offer resolution."

Celine and Julie were cuddling on the couch with plates of waffles balanced on their knees when the phone rang. Romeo/ Leo was crying hard for Juliet/Claire. It was such a beautiful fantasy of some alternate Miami. Palm trees and men with guns. Passionately literary men driving low riders. Celine whispered nauseous feelings with Shakespearean verve.

"Oh, apothecary! Thy medicine has made me sick this day, would I not long for sweet relief."

"You're such a dork."

Julie's mom came in. She opened a window. Celine watched her dark hair curling over her pink T-shirt, shoulders framed by textured white stucco wall. The light-green starburst of a spider plant caught in a web of morning light and shadow. Maybe it was the drugs, but the world looked like a painting. Town traffic came in and mixed with Leo's soliloquy.

"Girls," her hands quivered and her lips paled. Facing them, Julie's mom looked both beautiful and frightening. Like a crazy woman barely covering it up. "Could you turn that off?"

"Do we have to?" she sighed. And then she looked at her mother.

It wasn't new to see her with shiny eyes. Julie's mom tried to talk to the girls about emotions much more than Celine's mother. She would give them carrot sticks in the kitchen and ask what music they liked and how they experienced boys. She had once suggested they do a ceremony in the desert in honor of their periods. Julie in reaction never wanted to tell her anything. It wasn't unusual to see her mom crying, but at this moment, some deeper feelings seemed to be shaking her.

"What's wrong?"

"I just spoke to Debra. It's just a total tragedy. Horrible."

She was crying so intensely that there seemed to be no space in the room for other grief.

"Girls, I just want you. . . I don't want you to think this always happens. This is a total tragedy, but you can't live afraid."

"Mom. What happened?"

"Donna Beth died."

Neither of them felt anything but the clamminess of the other's hand and the fuzz of the blue blanket. Julie had not actually turned off *Romeo + Juliet*, just muted it. Leo as Romeo was dead and beautiful, just poisoned.

In the movie and the play, there was that tragic in-between space where he is alive but about to die and Juliet/Claire wakes up from her drugged state and they cross paths. The audience knows the whole of what the two characters know only partially. Juliet/Claire's plan has failed because Romeo/Leo did not know she was faking death. After they catch one another's anguished gaze, he really dies and she is left in the crypt with the boy she loves and his gun. Juliet/Claire takes the ivory handled gun. Her face crumpled in agony. She shoots herself and then they are symmetrical again. In the same dead state.

Julie's mom wiped her face, then wrapped her arms around herself. Julie remembered Donna Beth onstage in front of the theater's red velvet curtain. Tears.

Celine felt embarrassed mostly, as if she should not be there, but at home. If Julie was with her mother they could fall into the family space without judgment. But with Celine she had to maintain a distance.

There was so much space in the white room, with its quivering spider plant and its brown leather sofa. The red carpet showed vacuum marks and all their different footprints. Julie's mother kept crying. The girls began crying so that the mother could stop. They stayed like this until Julie's father came in and broke the spell.

21.

News of Donna Beth's murder spread like dust. Though Julie's mother hid the paper, the girls read it anyway, sitting side by side in the red vinyl coffee-shop booth. They ran their bitten nails over smudgy letters.

"Police have released more details of last Sunday's murder-suicide that left two women and one man dead. The 47-year-old woman and her 24-year-old daughter have been identified as Guadalupe Jackson and Donna Beth Gonzalez, both of Santa Teresa. The two were reportedly shot and killed by Jackson's estranged husband Frank Jackson, a member of US border patrol and resident of Sunland Park."

The next week there was a follow-up story. The journalist interviewed a criminologist from the university. This story, though a unique tragedy for the family, said the scholar, also fits into larger patterns of violence against women.

Pages swarmed with words. The girls felt so manic and depressed, raging and invisible. In conversation they whispered back and forth, trying to remake their understanding to fit new facts.

"Donna Beth, is," they repeated not believing, "dead."

"Murdered."

The girls and their families were invited to the memorial

service. It would be the second Julie had attended and the first for Celine.

The church Donna Beth's grandparents belonged to was newish, with wood panels, abstract stained glass, and blond carpet. Her grandmother and bald and red-eyed grandfather sat in two leather chairs in front of a curtain. Beside them was an easel with a department store portrait of Donna Beth and her mother. In the photo Donna Beth wore a demure baby-blue sweater and her mother wore lavender with a rose corsage pinned over her heart. The grandparents beside these photos appeared as if they were the dead, were aging right there, moving as quickly as they could from the brutality of curtains and carpets and strangers towards the time beyond.

The girls were struck by how dorky Donna Beth's extended family were when she had always been so poised, so cool. They spoke to her aunts, a dental hygienist in a navy blouse and a chubby nun in a polyester skirt. "So sorry for your loss."

The family was overwhelmed by Donna Beth's college friends. College actresses and actors and druggies and English majors and guitar players who had unwittingly been studying the beauty of grief for years filled the reception room and spilled onto the dry grass outside. Their battered black wing tips and long lace tunics were finally in the right setting. It seemed achingly right to be goth at a funeral. They cried, genuinely sad but also voluptuous in their capacity to feel this sadness. Even those who knew Donna Beth only casually felt stricken. They looked beautiful, crying and crying in tight black circles.

The biggest cloud of people formed around Donna Beth's boyfriend James. He was not crying. In this way he was like

Donna Beth's grandparents. Vacant. He was a drained boy in a black sweater and too big slacks, left wrecked and swaying by a middle-aged man's storm of rage. And that man, the murderer who'd torn through all these people with his gun, was the ghost who got to be there. Hovering in hate, he had created this murder play but then slipped out with his victims, so that revenge and forgiveness were impossible. How much hate there was.

Donna Beth's aunt gave Celine and Julie little cards with the Virgin Mary on one side and a prayer on the other.

A bouquet of beautiful memories,
sprayed with a million tears,
wishing God could have spared you,
if just for a few more years.
It does not take a special day,
for us to think of you,
each Mass we hear,
each prayer we say,
is offered up for you.
We cannot bring the old days back,
when we were all together,
our family chain is broken now,
but memories live forever.

Neither Celine nor Julie could cry, but their mothers did it for them.

Celine and Julie agreed events in their lives were intertwined. "Karma," they whispered. "Auspicious trines," they nodded. "Everything happens for a reason," they repeated.

On her birthday Julie ate mushrooms, not thinking her mother would want to take her out for cake. She was in bed, staring at the floral curtains. It did not occur to Julie to refuse her mother, but she thought of hiding in the bathroom. Her high eyes could hide behind sunglasses in the car, but what about after?

They ordered apple pie and peppermint tea. Her mom kept asking about theater and her feelings. Because she was pretty high she could not keep the words in. They spilled out as a Mardi Gras necklace of words. She said too much. She said, "One night, Julie and I were alone and I don't even know what happened, but hell came to the window. I could hear one hundred and fifty trillion spirits pressed against the window, all around the bush for the hummingbirds. And so I got up, it was horrifying."

Her mother just smiled with teary eyes, sipping her tea. After a while in the too big, almost empty coffee shop her mother asked if she'd like to go across the street to the music/book/video superstore. Julie wondered what that meant.

"Yes," she said.

A green carpet like in a hotel lobby, like in a chain restaurant. She wandered into the alternative music section. Alternative. Keep spinning eyes down. Find something recognizable.

It made no sense or rather, it was so mystical, and therefore right. She handed the CD with the cover image of a girl amid flowers to her mother and said, confidant her mother would understand the cosmic significance, "This CD has my name on it!"

That night, coming down, she told Celine, who agreed but also rolled her eyes, "But of course it was there with your name on it. You special ordered it last week, you idiot."

"Yes, but I forgot I ordered it. What are the chances I would find it, while on mushrooms, on my birthday? It was magic."

"Okay, but maybe you felt it was a little that way because you were tripping."

"You're just jealous."

"You're right. While you were high shopping for magical CDs, I was studying *War and Peace*."

"Be nice to me. I'm still high."

"You know I love you. Happy birthday?"

"Be nice, Celine, because I love you."

23.

Without realizing it or even trying they got to the end of high school. Celine graduated early and started classes at the local college in January. Just sort of slid in. Julie finished on time and with an easy 4.0. It didn't require effort. She didn't bother attending graduation. Her father said it was up to her. She started with some summer school classes, Early American History and Intro to French. The college classes were more interesting, but not much harder than what she'd encountered before. Deep concentration felt impossible in the heat, so the girls spent their time stoned and wandering. It felt like a blurry transition, not a fresh start. Their only cause for excitement was that Celine got an apartment.

In Celine's apartment they made impromptu exaggerated choreographies to that song from *Pulp Fiction*, "Girl, You'll Be a Woman Soon." Julie was jealous of the apartment, but her parents told her to save her money.

At the Goodwill they hunted for the right '70s cowboy shirt to pair with new Calvin Kleins, jeans so expensive they could never tell their moms. They saved the best outfits for fall. Over the summer they experimented with layered tanks with bra straps showing, the edge of the shirt not meeting the waistband of the floral skirt. The flesh of the world of the exposed hip.

They'd go to parties late. Curfew ceased to exist because of Celine's place.

Miguel was still around, ambiguously there. Being insatiable, each time Julie saw Miguel she had to keep from saying, I want more. Julie could not contain the feeling of Miguel. She wrote his name. She wrote it on her hand. In love, she thought, carefully avoiding barer facts. She called him one time at his dad's. "I slept with this girl at a party," he said. "Oh," she said, but not more. "Don't worry, it's not that serious." She cried all night without letting her parents hear. She stopped herself from calling him, but he didn't stop and she ended up taking the calls.

At eighteen they finally felt like performers rather than audience. Julie decided to be vegetarian. Celine did too. They related to animals. Soft, big-eyed things that people hurt without thinking. The difference between their beloved cats and a sheep or cow seemed a matter of scale, not type. They talked about everyone's callousness in the face of suffering.

They watched the girls with pierced tongues who wrote checks their emotions couldn't cash. You know what that piercing says to boys, don't you? Big eyes popping almost out of the skull.

Celine and Julie learned how it felt when a boy held their hair back when they felt sick. They learned how it felt when boys pulled their hair during a blow job. It was not unwanted, this attention, though they also learned that guilt came with all this. It was a time of learning.

On the bank of the Rio Grande they noticed a Dr. Pepper Bonne Bell Lip Smackers crushed into the dirt. It was that one sunset when they were there smoking a joint. The sky was going soft pink and blue and swallows were flying mad patterns to catch insects above the river.

24.

The theater staged *Marat/Sade*, a play within a play set in a madhouse. The girls were finally old enough to be the actresses they had watched.

Julie was cast as the narcoleptic murderer Charlotte Corday; Celine was cast as a patient.

The director was a guest artist from England. His accent made his statements theatrical and profound. When the director was hanging around before rehearsal, Celine felt she could see him as something less than brilliant. Silent, she could see him as just a bony man with wispy hair the color of a quail, staring at undergrad girls. In rehearsal, though, he lectured over their heads. The girls wrote notes with lots of question marks.

Leftists. Marat stabbed in the bathtub by narcoleptic

Charlotte. It gives de Sade a hard-on, or everything does or nothing does save for throwing a woman into a volcano. Napoleon, bread and insanity, pleasure's proximity to pain, David, communists, the atomic bomb, the Algerian War, flows of refugees, political martyrdoms, slogans and chants, transgression, the question, presentation and representation, Brecht and Artaud, guilt and freedom, sexual social position, democracy and its others, the abuse of power, mass violence, destruction of being in the name of being. The play was nested within a history the small-town cast strained to imagine. The director extemporized on perpetual revolution, folded into reference within reference. Julie wrote notes as Celine teared up, letting his words wash over her. He talked glory, horror, and sacrifice. Peter Brook in his production insisted that the actors immerse themselves in madness.

The director explained, "We're talking about a time before drugs or treatment. People didn't think the mad were fully human." He brought in pictures of Goya and showed them *Titicut Follies*. He insisted the white costumes be dirtier and argued with the lighting designer about the patterns dappling the stage. Everyone in the play caught the same excitement. They thought what they were making was profound and political.

The director lectured the college kids about historical memory and revolution. He made them catatonic and manic figures, drooling and scratching from trauma.

"These are the first modern men and women," he shouted as they improvised movement. "Look at them, marked with tattoos, starved, addicted, and prone to random violence. Then look at each other. You are incapable of remembering one moment to the next, and so you are reduced to living in a hollow present. None but Marat can remember his lines, but what of that? He's a man covered in sores, confined to a bath. He declaims as if he's on the speaker's corner of the dead. This is your revolution? Only de Sade understands history. Only de Sade has the strength to show the subliminal horror and desire of the modern world. And where is he, you ask? He is right here in this godforsaken desert with all you maniacs. Drag yourself, you shit, you syphilitic beauties. He'll violate you whenever he wants."

The director forced the college musicians—awkward kids a few seasons removed from high school marching band—to clang their bodies into their instruments as if war was coming.

"This bathhouse is Auschwitz! This netherworld is a prison in Palestine! It is a classroom in Chernobyl! Whatever realm of horror you can conjure in your pretty little heads, go there. You are acting in a place of functionary horror. Know that when you get offstage you'll be force-fed sedatives and bound to a bed. A war is coming whether you see it our not, a war has already begun."

He had them pour buckets of blood during the guillotine sequence. This was a rip-off of the Peter Brook production, but it didn't matter. It still worked. They were thrilled every time they did it.

"You are the inmate survivors from the last revolution and now, here for this silly moment, you are allowed to chant for your one real desire. A new revolution to free you from the one just passed.

"Say it with me. Tell me what you want."

"Revolution?"

"Tell me, when do you want it?"

"Now?"

"Say it again with your hearts. What do you want?"

The cast screamed again like it was real.

25.

One day, four weeks into their five-week rehearsal, Celine sat in bed drinking coffee and half-doing homework for her political science course. She'd left the radio on, so Chopin or someone was playing in the kitchen. Freedom felt like reading in pajamas. Class wasn't until noon.

The reading was about the crimes of Pinochet's government. Nerves vibrated from the coffee and the details of the world, rats and electrical wires, stadiums full of students and activists. The book described, very matter-of-factly, disappearances and the torture of sweet-looking leftist students and citizens. She started crying, calmed herself, started reading again and got to the part about the CIA's involvement. There was a photo of Nixon, her parents' historical monster. There was Henry Kissinger in black and white smiling next to Pinochet. Our government encouraged and facilitated and only pretended not to know. She looked up the word 'complicity' in the dictionary.

Doesn't matter what her mother said. The forefathers did so crucify people. Earlier in the semester she'd read about how Coke factories contracted paramilitary soldiers to throw union organizers out of helicopters into green jungles below. CIA involvement in South American conflicts was not a theory, she thought. A number of conspiracies overlapped. Something is not a conspiracy theory if it actually occurred. Did people know about this? How could people act like life was okay if this were the truth? It was unbearable. She felt confused and furious.

She went into the kitchen to make toast. On the radio the concerto had been replaced by low, concerned news voices describing a teenage disaster. She sat and listened as the reporter described a chaotic array of details about a school massacre in a western Colorado town. Ski masks and semiautomatics, SWAT teams and mud. Kids murdered in the library. The president had called a hasty press conference and she heard his voice say, "We must reach out to our young people, we must teach them to resolve their anger with words not weapons." She began crying and for the rest of the day felt teary.

That night in rehearsal, the director talked about glory, horror, and sacrifice, so that this cast of students could physically communicate something abstract about states and violence and people living in states of exception.

"You and I and all of us, we are cracking this surface. The audience that comes to opening night doesn't yet know they need what you have to say. They might not know, but that doesn't matter. It is your job to give them these transmissions from the past. It is your job to remind them that the mad, the hopeless and wild, the oppressed and hated, are as human as they are. There but for the grace of God. It is your job to find the light and hit the mark, project to the back of the house. It is your job to sing as if you are about to be marched to the stadium and shot dead. Make them feel because you feel. Fill silences with the knowledge that you'll be tortured after the curtain call and they must put themselves on the line to stop these violences from endlessly cycling.

"Are you ghosts or the living? Are you free or institutionalized?

Which side are you on, boys," the director laughed then added, "and girls? Which side are you on?

"Don't tell the audience," said the director. "Show them your humanity."

26.

The girls wandered around Julie's parents' house like ghosts. Her parents were away for the weekend, so they had access to the large TV and nice stereo. "No parties" was all her mom had said.

Celine tried on Julie's velvet skirt. She twisted around to hide the Band-Aid on her hip. Julie saw, but didn't mention it.

They ate Wheat Thins and ice cream. After much deliberation they decided Julie would call Miguel. Celine listened to one side of the phone conversation.

"Don't be mean to me, Miguel. I'm so sweet to you, you jerk."

Through the open window they heard drunks getting into a confused fight about some car.

Julie showed Celine how to inhale above the blue flame burner. Smoke hotter and more acrid than imagined. Painful coughing followed by laughing, followed by whiff of singed hair and wet grass out the open window.

"Hold in for a long time."

Followed by Celine's brain balling up, a wet scarf. It had been raining. Somehow her face was wrapped in the scarf. To extract self from self proved difficult. Celine had in her hand a SeaWorld mug.

"Is this whale real?"

"Real how?

"Like a tiny whale?"

"Shame on you Shamu."

"If I could just get around front and see the whole picture." Celine laughed, throwing her voice. Eyes on her skirt, her lap of pink velvet.

"I think I'm dying." There was a hand on the pillow, or a model of a hand, her own hand. Pretty convincing.

Miguel's car appeared in the driveway, then Miguel was at the door and he and Julie were laughing at Celine or maybe just laughing.

"I think I'm dead."

Somebody had turned on the TV.

"What is black and white and somehow familiar?"

"Julie, Jule, J, J J J remember this? Haven't we seen it before?"

On screen a horseman with a knife gouged out the eyes of a struggling man. Celine saw the couch in the dark, saw Julie and Miguel tangled up with arms up T-shirts sleeves and around necks. Making out, but too confused by buttons and seams.

"Why do they have to murder the animals, Julie? I don't understand. Julie?"

"God, I'm changing this. You girls are too emotional, always." Miguel switched channels to the chaotic color of music video, then slid down to the floor. He moved his hands slowly onto both girls' legs, grinning but without looking at them. Hands moving slowly—but quite perceptibly to their nervous systems— under their skirts. Julie sighed and stroked Celine's hair.

"Julie?"

"Celine. Sweetheart. Girl. Shut up."

Julie kissed Celine a little, but then Miguel took to kissing them both and he moved his hands more insistently inside them. It felt so sweet and reasonable with the drugs. He made them both come and then sat between them, cuddling and tripping out to the headlights climbing up and down the walls, entering and leaving through the picture window one after another.

After hours they all fell into wired half-sleep. When, a few hours later, morning light began playing off the picture window, Miguel woke Julie. "Quiet," he said and pulled her towards her parents' bedroom.

How things move from kissing to more. He wrapped his hands around the back of her head. To want to give in, to give in. His belt buckle against her cheek. This change of perspective. Head down. Choking reduced her world to a manageable size. He kept her head going with one ear pressed into his hipbone until he came, slapping caressing at the end.

"Bye, sweetheart." She listened to his car door shut and engine start.

27.

Julie felt disenchanted. She'd learned of the concept in her literary theory class and it seemed to apply to her whole being. She stumbled on the phone with Celine.

"Just fuck it."

"What?"

"Just . . . everything."

To become an actress would keep her forever in the object realm, forever guided by an outside hand. There had to be a way out, or over, or through. All the bridges had been constructed with shoddy material. But you use what's available, and the truth was she was a girl with resources to escape. She was lucky. She just had to actually use her luck to get out.

Julie convinced her parents to let her transfer to Portland State University. She hadn't taken out any student loans yet and she was at least partway through, she argued. She'd done everything right and even started school early, she guilted. She had an aunt in that city, she reasoned. She needed to leave the desert and Miguel, all this psychic dark, she cried. Her mother caved, and after that her father demurred. He made her fill out the FAFSA while he watched. A month housesitting was arranged, friends of family friends.

"Julie is responsible and loves cats," her mother assured.

A plane ticket was bought on Southwest. Her life suddenly had a new frame.

28.

Celine and Julie stood next to the river looking towards the mountains, watching the sunset like good romantics. They could not help but notice how dense the atmosphere was. It was written that once the whole West was clear and sage-scented, with an intangible sky-blown, sun-shot, sublime atmosphere. You breathed it in without feeling it; you saw through it a hundred miles and the image did not blur.

The border was there in the distance, forgettable for those on the American side because it was so fortified yet porous when they wanted it to be. It was a ruled line of wire mesh, steel posts, floodlights, and a concrete trench. The Texas officials liked to talk about how their city was one of the safest in the nation.

Each quarter mile an officer sat in an SUV all night with headlights beaming. Each morning their replacement arrived with Flying J coffee and breakfast burritos wrapped in silver foil paper. The officers maintained constant radio contact. By magic or design, they expected disaster. To expect is to call into being.

"Come visit," Julie begged.

"I don't know if I can get the money," Celine wept.

"Well, write me, call me. We're still best friends. That's never going to change."

Two girls on the edge held one another's arms. Before their eyes, the line of the border wavered, appearing to disappear. One turned to the other to whisper.

"Don't tell, show. We are navigating folding, unfolding time. We have heard it before, it bears repeating. This is all a play within a play set in a madhouse. A play about the sounds rabbits make when dying. We are all whores, shadows who meet the moment."

The one listening nodded.

Night fell over itself to get to the horizon, rendering them invisible. Far off a pair of headlights crested a hill and bobbed over the bad ground. The sunlight was totally gone from the sky, and by the time the headlights swept the scene next to the river, the girls who had been there were gone.

29.

After Julie left, Celine cried many times a day. She also went out more. She thought nobody could tell how sad she was. Celine doubted there would ever be a time in her life without regular bouts of crying.

She thought that no one cared how she felt anyway. At parties she was bubblier than she had been when she'd had Julie. She told jokes she would have let her best friend deliver.

On the 4th of July she went to a pool party at somebody's parents' house. A table with guacamole, chip bags, and greasy plates. There was so much drinking. Boys pushed girls into the pool.

"Viva," somebody shouted. Two pit bulls play-fought in a penned-off area of the dirt yard.

"I feel like," a girl mumbled, "I learned about sex and death first through my pets."

"On my tenth birthday neighbor dogs killed my rabbit."

"Oh poor mi hijita!"

"Shutupasshole. It was traumatic."

Celine thought back to the memory of her cat bawling in heat. Another night, after the cat had been fixed, she'd forced it to stay in bed with her under the covers while she plugged her ears to try to block out the moaning of her parents having sex.

"Do you want to get high?" High and drunk already mixed. It was getting dark when a handful of them climbed onto the roof. July was the rainy season and often the fireworks competed with far-off displays of lightning.

"Where's your girlfriend, Celine?"

"Wait, are you really gay?" Hysterical laughter.

"Fuck off."

"Viva!" a girl with sparklers whooped as lightning flashed over the mountains.

Celine took in the fireworks without thinking of them. Her vision blurred. Maybe she let her eyes unfocus. Shimmering spiderwebs followed explosions, tracers, distant crackles and bangs. Gold and black. Think of gold and black shaken together with streaks and pops, disappearing into one another faster than you can focus on. Think about blur of gold and black, silver and smoke. From rooftops and backyards people hooted. There was a scattering of gunshots and consumer-grade fireworks complementing the ones from the city going off over the stadium.

It got late. This dude who was familiar, a friend of somebody's friend named Bobby or Jimi or Juan or something, was like, earnestly going to town on his acoustic guitar. My God, Celine thought, why am I still here? But still she stayed. There was nothing but her empty apartment to go back to and no work tomorrow.

In the hallway waiting for the bathroom, she wondered if she was too fucked up to drive.

"Well look who it is."

She hadn't seen Miguel since that time at Julie's. He looked a little more solid and glassy eyed than before, but it was summer and a holiday weekend, so. He smiled in a way that precluded an awkward talk. He took the control as she gave it.

"You behaving yourself?"

"Guess so."

They ended up in the backyard in two lawn chairs. The party thinned, but those still there took up more space. The boys worked to drink all the remaining alcohol. Someone found a bottle of Baileys. God. The girls were girlfriends.

I'm just staying to sober up, Celine reminded herself. She backed this up with a red plastic cup of water that tasted of tequila.

Miguel said he hadn't been up too much, just fucking around.

Celine said, "Mmmhmm."

Miguel asked, "Did you watch the news today? It's kind of crazy, I guess. You know my buddy Jeff? The one who does graffiti? So like he's doing something, some art thing."

"He's so cute."

"I'll tell him you said so."

"Miguel! Don't! Be nice. But anyway, tell me what happened?"

"So he's been stealing pieces of billboards with graffiti on them. I've gone with him a few times. We'd drive out on the frontage road, make sure there were no cops. Climb up with his tools and grab the piece. Easy right?

"So we'd been drinking. Jeff started telling me about this sick tag up on a truck stop billboard. He's into this project and says it's a big deal with some sculptor up in Santa Fe. So he's excited and I'm like, fuck it. We had no business driving anywhere, but so it goes. It was late late.

"We drive towards the mountains. He's excited. We get out of the car, climb the ladder and get to work unscrewing this panel. I don't know what I'm doing with tools, but he does. He's handy like that. I am fucked up, but clear too. You know how tequila makes you?

"So Jeff is doing the hard stuff and I'm spacing out, waiting for him on my back, looking at the sky. Then there was this horrible noise. We froze.

"I don't know if you can picture it, but there's the frontage road where our car was parked behind a wall. Then there's the highway, and on the other side of that, a whole subdivision. So where we were we could see the scene, but those on the highway couldn't see us.

"There had been an accident. I'm going to guess drunk driving because it was just, you know. It was this little motorcycle and a Toyota truck, head-on. Just shattered. And it was all spread out like a movie shot in front of Jeff and I under those yellow highway lights. Glass and parts of the bike, stuff from inside the truck, like tools, garbage. The motorcycle just wrapped around the truck. Shredded, oil and rubber skid marks along the road.

"Because it was so late, or early, no other cars came for a little while. I don't know. Maybe three or four minutes. Both of us were high and drunk as fuck, but also maybe in shock or something. Finally Jeff snaps out of it. 'We should go help them.' But it was clear. Like the motorcyclist did not survive. His body was thrown or crushed. I don't know. It was bad.

"And we don't see the driver. So for a minute we're like, what should we do? We should climb down. We should go call the police. In that time there are lights, sirens. Maybe somebody in one of the houses called. Something. So then, we feel trapped up there. Breaking the law, drunk driving. Stealing a piece of a billboard. How are we going to explain ourselves, right? And Jeff is already on probation because of graffiti. So we're up there. Hiding, I guess. And we don't know what we could tell them anyway. So we just watched."

"Miguel. Oh my God."

"I know, right? So we're up there and it's even getting a little light over the mountains. Like this soft light. Beautiful. My brain just sort of sped up and then slowed way down. The air was super-crisp but soft. We agree silently. We couldn't crawl down. So we watched. Watched the police walk around. Close the road. In the distance traffic backed up a little. Another set of lights flashes at the WalMart exit. The ambulance was there. The truck driver bleeding out of his head. We could see it when they took him into the ambulance. And the motorcyclist. I will remember this to the day I die. Swear to God. They covered the body with this sheet and the whole sheet turned red. It just seeped and seeped. Jeff and I just watched the stain spread. We couldn't have done a thing."

"Are you okay?"

"Sure," Miguel said, all flat, before a last chug of Modelo.

"I think Jeff is more fucked up than I am. But one thing's for sure. I'm never going to drink and drive ever again." He laughed dark at the open secret, saying what he didn't believe. Celine leaned in and hugged him. He bunched his shoulders, then softened. The hug went long. He took the back of her head and kissed her, pushed his tongue into her mouth. They kissed more and more while he moved his hands around her body. She felt his dick harden against her leg. She couldn't help it. She let out a little sigh. She closed her eyes against the chaotic pattern inside.

"Fuck," he laughed slowly as he pushed her away, "you're like my little sister. I got to go. You take care of yourself. If you talk to Julie, send her my love."

She went into the bathroom quick. Hoping most of all that no one had seen them. Julie was all the way inside her mind.

When Celine left the party Miguel had some girl pressed into a corner of the sofa, all falling hair over face and hands on neck. Driving home in tears she swore to herself and the sky, I'm leaving too, even if it kills me. That was the last time she ever saw Miguel.

2.

Bad Manors

30.

Summer in the Northwest came later and more gently than on the border. It was May, then June, and Julie still needed a sweater. After her house-sitting gig, Julie sublet from a woman who was backpacking across Europe. She loved her temporary room with its two walls of windows made of small panes of glass. She loved the view into a muddy backyard and a flowering then leafy apple tree. She slept beneath the absent woman's velvet quilt and read all her Kundera novels. It was intoxicating.

For the first weeks she walked everywhere, across town and through weird city blind spots where only the homeless and crazies walked. The neighborhoods consisted of dilapidated mansions wreathed in irises, roses, and wildflowers. Community gardens patchworked empty lots. Blackberries grew over overgrown alley weeds. When she eventually bought a yellow Schwinn at the Salvation Army it was so ancient and heavy that walking was still easier, so she still walked.

Her first West Coast friend was a semi-feral girl from Boston. They bonded out of need. She scared Julie, but also fascinated her. Jen worked at a bagel store, had a septum piercing, shoplifted, didn't apparently give a fuck about much, and knew about all the good music shows.

Julie followed like a trusting fool. They squished into the back seat of strangers' cars, hung out in backyard parties someone's someone had maybe been invited to, drinking beers and offering dollars to whoever would buy more. She trusted she would be okay. The insanity of this trust was clear only in retrospect. But she was okay.

One night Jen invited Julie over. After wandering and a trip to Baskin-Robbins they returned to Jen's to find two men hanging with her roommates. The men looked out of place beside the skateboarder boys who were all loose gestures and jeans. The two had creases at the mouth and the hairy arms of grown men. They seemed hard. Jen bounced around. One of the men sat close to Julie. To be polite she asked about his snake-knife-pinup girl tattoo.

"It's for my ex-wife," he said. Julie's mind reeled with the implications. She got quiet.

But then one of these guys said, as if the question were natural, "You all want some meth?"

So they all smoked meth and Julie was more curious about experience than she was willing to concede to good sense. By chance that was the last time she ever saw Jen.

Julie got a job at a gourmet pizza restaurant downtown. The customers were insufferable men and women in business casual who often became angry about the slow delivery of their wild mushroom pie or the temperature of their Perrier. She developed a crush on Lukas the pizza chef after getting stoned with him and their neurotic but funny manager after closing one night.

Then it was July and there were fireworks and enough heat to warrant swimming. Julie hung out with her borrowed roommates—an Irish guy who worked at the youth hostel, a carpenter, a cooking student, and a film student with buckteeth doing a photo documentary on queers in the Northeast.

She got to ride in Derek or Anne or Corey's car while they all joked and got high and played tapes of Desmond Decker, Elliott Smith, De La Soul. The Dandy Warhols' record gave her a headache, she protested. Derek made her a mixtape and they'd listen to that.

They would swim before a show or a party, where Julie would flirt like she'd seen the actresses flirt back home. These guys were of a different order from Miguel. She flirted with twenty-five-year-olds with design or bartending jobs who were getting over for-real ex-girlfriends. More than a couple of times she surprised herself when her techniques worked and she ended up thousands of miles from home in a strange man's car, living room, bed, kissing and whatever.

Then one time Lukas invited her home. He was all sinew and tattoo. He gave Julie a hard orgasm while she looked and closed her eyes so as not to look at his poster-covered walls and ceiling. There was *The Exorcist, Reservoir Dogs,* and an action shot of Tony Montana in his Hawaiian shirt, gunning down people out of the frame. The sex hurt, not because he meant it to, but because he was tightly wound. Hip bone ground into hip. After he came, they lay there for a little while he smoked and told her how he'd been harassed in London for his dreadlocks. He decided to cut them because they began to feel like "a punk prop."

They had sex two other times, his bony fingers pushed without sensitivity inside her. Then him on top or behind her. Julie felt as if she were acting someone else's part. She remembered Miguel licking her fingers so soft. After, Lukas would smoke and talk about home and music.

The last time, just when he'd pushed inside her, his girlfriend or ambiguous ex, Johanna—who was a grown woman—walked into his bedroom.

In horror Julie met her gaze.

Johanna asked in a cool monotone, "Seriously?" before turning and walking right back out.

He leapt up and into his jeans in one motion. Gone.

Alone in his bed, all wet and cold-hot, Julie lay for a long while studying the demonic Linda Blair's green skin and half-cocked eyes.

Finally she pulled on her panties and dress. Lukas came back in, put an arm around her shoulders and said, "I'm afraid we've been acting stupid, kid."

It wasn't even late. She walked back to her sublet where the roommates were just getting ready for a Fugazi show. Someone had an extra ticket. Did she want to go? Sure. The summer was almost over.

31.

In an empty house Julie took a pregnancy test. Her anxiety played tricks. It was negative. Of course it was. As soon as she saw, she launched into internal criticism about wasting fifteen dollars on a plastic thing you pee on.

School was starting in a week. She decided it was time to take the drugs she'd been saving. Squishing the mushrooms into a ginger candy masked their noxious flavor.

She washed her face while waiting for them to take effect. "Is This Desire?" played on repeat. She called Celine, but her answering machine picked up and she didn't know what message to leave, so she hung up.

I wish you were here. Have I been a bad friend? Do you miss me? Do I even exist?

Uncontrollable crying turned funny. God, this is stupid. She went into the backyard and stood beneath the apple tree. She went back inside, changed her shirt and panties. Had her jeans ever felt this comfortable? It was so fine. She took a multivitamin.

Sitting outside again with the sound of the neighbor's dinner party floating over the fence, she wrote Celine a letter she would never end up mailing. Still, it was cathartic. Then she wrote to Miguel. She poured her emotion into that letter, the feelings that got stuck in her nineteen-year-old shoulders and head. It was love and violent love—if that meant seeing another person as fully human, independent of what she wanted, wished, or needed. She could for that moment see those two people as full, real, complex humans. How could there be this much love in her?

After the letters she was really high and the leaves looked dipped in seawater. Tomato plants toppled over mint sprigs. God, how lovely. She took some photos on a disposable point-and-shoot. She lay still and allowed hidden nausea to surface alongside vague cathartic realizations. She left the home that was not her home with some deep relaxed faith that she would be okay. She was protected—by what, she didn't know—but the belief had to be enough.

32

Neither girl kept with theater. They didn't keep with one another either. Without meaning to they fell out of touch, but thought of one another tenderly. Cryptic postcards arrived to various addresses. One would call and leave an effusive message. Another would call and a roommate would answer. "Celine called for Julie" would appear on a chalkboard beside a chore wheel before another roommate would erase it so there was room to write "We need dish soap and rice." They were two versions of a kind of girl, similar in form but split in space and mostly unaware of their other's doings. Sleep followed waking followed sleep followed waking, and thus, friends moved away from one another. Their passions ran along parallel tracks invisible to them.

While Celine stuck it out in the desert for a while longer, Julie finished college in the Northwest. A few years later, at graduation, Julie smiled a thin smile for her father's camera. She dressed in her vintage best and posed beside her mother, who wore a linen blouse and a cut-velvet scarf. Julie was accepted to a film studies program in Vancouver. Family friends smiled approvingly. Canada, people told her, was kinder, prettier, and more peaceful. No guns and no political bullying, her English professor enthused. They're civilized there.

Their country had just begun its newest amorphous war, which like others before it revolved around revenge and greed. Both girls attended big protests on the same day in different parts of the continent.

After Celine finished college she traveled cross-country and ended up in New York. She walked all around the financial district in a fog, imagining the damp swirls were full of poisonous particulates.

She drifted, picking up and dropping jobs as a hostess, baker, camp councillor, and photographer's assistant—all to save up money for backpacking in Europe.

A few days in London and Paris, then to an organic farm near Lelystad, where she froze her fingers cutting lettuce predawn. In Spain her wisdom teeth came in and her parents told her to just pay for their removal on her credit card; they would help her out, they sighed. Checking the Internet on a youth-hostel computer in Porto, she saw the Abu Ghraib photos for the first time.

Julie and Celine mirrored one another unconsciously in the books they read and the secondhand cashmeres and mod miniskirts they favored. They modeled new lives. Both Celine and Julie put deserts behind them, convincing themselves it was just a corrupted cowboy land—a myth world cast in violet light—which they were now safely out of. The real world felt brutal, yes, but also so beautifully visible, and they were finally in it.

33.

Julie grew accustomed to the reaction. When she'd say Vancouver, many would let out a familiar sigh.

"It's so magical there!"

At first Julie thought she would love the city as she had Portland.

It was the glossier version of the Pacific Northwest. It had money and highlighted hair and organic bamboo hoodies and oyster happy hours. It had overgrown leftist communal houses giving way to empty lots slated for condo-development. Rain glazed the glass skyscrapers. This city was the hottest urban body Canada could sculpt, rubbing up against old-growth woods. It had won an Olympic bid and attracted the global gaze.

She was moving through the future. She took a ferry and saw actual orcas jumping together like on a tourism pamphlet. A new friend took her for California rolls and sake. They strolled the seawall eating chai gelato.

After a month in a Craigslist hippie sublet, she lucked into a rare affordable studio apartment in a boarding house nicknamed Bad Manors. The bathrooms and showers were in the hall, shared by her, a band guy, and an old man who told her once in the laundry room that his cat was his only friend, but whatever. The little place belonged just to her and overlooked a beautiful park where handsome skateboarders practiced tricks. It was the edge of fall. She felt fresh and eager to make herself a real scholar.

34.

Julie's new classmates introduced themselves by talking hermeneutics and Habermas. They dressed in designer jeans and band T-shirts. Deleuze had a specific generational appeal. Those who most loved talking rhizomes tended to be men in work jackets and sporty kicks and square glasses with some bright accent like a line of electric blue. She noticed these guys often used the phrase "as such."

She belonged to another subculture of subcultural critics. She studied Baudelaire and Benjamin, Kafka and Kracauer, read of nineteenth- and twentieth-century degradation and paranoia. The style tended more towards interwar than postwar, German rather than French, but the cool Germans who fled their homeland. Her clique liked decay and utopia, Bataille and Marker, haptic cinema and affect theory. The aesthetic was downers not uppers, excavation and decay not demolition and rebuilding, thrift not tech, the idea of Detroit not the idea of Beijing, a messianic view of history not a perverse embrace of the singularity. Color-coded Post-its fattened her books.

Of course. Of course these shifting groups agreed—at various art shows, readings, and in classes—there were not only two choices. Binary thinking was oppressive and destroys the productive intrapersonal dialogic gray space, they agreed. There was much to think about.

Julie stayed up late nights blowing smoke out her window into the rain. New ideas filled cups and teapots. Her bedsheets became nest-like with tangled sheets that smelled. The unmade bed smelled grassy from her chamomile essential oils and incense burning. She slept in, dreaming of Escher interiors. For breakfast she soft-boiled eggs, sautéed spinach, spread grainy toast with quince jam while listening to Arthur Russell.

Julie worked hard to join ranks of intellectuals gone before. She kept thinking about all the work that people had never made. The unwritten notations for dances never performed. In the lulls between traffic she imagined the sounds of music never played. It was the music she came to prefer. Unmade art, she came to think, was the most beautiful. What is the closest thing to nothing at all? Monochromes, drones, she decided, glances and stutters, dust and clouds, failures and gaps. Satie,

Young, Cage. So many brilliant people have not done so little. All this almost absence put pushy meaning to shame.

Her kitchen table was one of those '50s Formica-topped ones, covered in little stars. She rarely saw the stars because the whole thing was covered with books: *The Bonds of Love, Dreamworld and Catastrophe, Guilty Pleasures, On Longing, The Artificial Kingdom, The Poetics of Space, Debbie: An Epic.*

Her time moved in slow builds, greedy bursts of studying followed by lackadaisical periods of hanging out, recovery sleep, and too much drinking. Her notebook filled with quotes because she thought handwriting was the best way to absorb what others wrote. After a paper was done the subtle connections between the quotations became obscure. Each semester was a push to the edge of her sense of sense.

Her essays were supposed to be specific and carefully argued, informed by texts, but spiked with original insight. Over time she came to both love that way of working and to see it as a trap. She labored over an essay on a film about two women in comas who were tended by men who spent their time talking to one another and crying.

She wrote, "In order to participate and be seen, women are required to submit their bodies and psyches to social manipulation. They are pure bodies without the conscious will to move themselves. So they are moved. They are talked to and talked for, but do not speak themselves."

Her professor said her ideas had promise, but she needed to keep working on clarity.

35

She read the story and it was like the bleakest Grimms' fairy tale. It happened in a beautiful land, on the western edge of a large and prosperous country. It happened in a small city a short way from the big city. Urban development or sprawl had physically connected the two over the past fifty years, though in terms of jurisdiction and feel they were separate entities. The residents saw themselves as members of a wholesome community rooted in industry and farming. They were rural and working-class in mindset, but only a short drive from illicit temptations and only a good real estate deal away from the top tax bracket.

In this place a farmer and a farmer's wife bore a child who grew up and found a wife. Together they raised three children: a daughter and two sons. They sent the girl away to boarding school, but raised their boys on the farm, surrounded by its smells and cycles of birth and slaughter.

When the parents died, the girl and two boys sold some farmland to a developer and in that way became quite rich. People wanted new schools and subdivisions and parking lots and parks. Land was valuable not for the quality of its soil but for how many units it could bear.

The two boys, left with small parcels of land and large bank accounts, continued to live farm lives, though it was now not career but hobby.

One brother turned his holdings into a nonprofit society with the mission of raising money for sports organizations and worthy community groups. He hosted dances, concerts, formal and casual recreations in the tin shed on Burns Road. Corn and potato salad, roast pork and hotdogs, watermelon and sheet cakes, beers and sodas were laid out on long tables.

Mayors and city council members, business and community leaders, mothers and fathers visited. In the extended twilights of Canadian summer, children roamed the grounds.

Despite community support the place was dogged by rumors about a dark side. Besides fundraisers, this man was said to host looser affairs for local hustlers. Hell's Angels, longshoremen, pimps, dealers, petty criminals, and prostitutes came to the farm on off-nights

There were the same roast pigs and corn and beer, but there were also liquor, drugs, and spare beds.

The wealthy farmer could afford to be a sugar daddy. He could buy and consume what he wanted.

One thing he did not buy though was meat. Though he could afford not to, he raised the pigs and butchered them himself as a hobby. The pigs were not his sole farming activity—he had a vegetable garden and chickens and goats—but the pigs became a macabre leitmotif of the story. He became known only as a pig farmer when he became known.

36.

Julie tried to resist the spectacle of the pig farmer serial killer case. Her impulse was to look away, but she found she couldn't. The facts stared out from newspapers left at coffee shops. She drank her cappuccino and tried not to look, but did. The paper printed the names of his victims beneath tiny pictures of them in rows, like yearbook shots.

In the morning as she ironed a shirt and waited for the weather forecast, the radio news voices discussed the women. After years of uninvestigated rumors, dismissed missing persons reports, and even a stabbing incident, this farmer was formally accused of many murders. As the details of the case emerged, it became clear that the story was one of a serial killer who targeted women on the margins, women who traversed prostitution and drug scenes, the hyper-visible yet willfully overlooked. This bad man tugged the frayed edges of the urban cloth, slipping in and out of the holes. For a long time he could get away with it.

When they said 'dismemberment,' Julie would switch off the radio and pick up her umbrella or bike helmet. Days it was expected to rain, she walked; on clear ones, she biked. Her path to the downtown campus unavoidably led through the neighborhood where the farmer had picked up all those girls.

37.

Her friends from the city had a studied way of shrugging with concern. It wasn't that they didn't care; it was that the Downtown Eastside had been a tangle of problems for forever. The used condoms and syringes that dotted the alleys were metonyms for a whole web of toxic choices made by Vancouver people. Choice and the absence of choice. For them this new horror twisted into the long-running saga that had parts for mayors and real estate developers, housing activists and shop-keepers, small-time dealers, hurt teens, and residential school survivors.

Within the community of artists and academics, there were other layers of emotion and dialogue. Reactions ranged from rage to depression to polite indifference to a shielding of the eyes as they walked the main drag on their way between an art opening and their favorite Szechuan restaurant. People in her classes related it to Baudelaire's poems, to the mechanization of the body, to Agamben's conception of bare life under neoliberal world order. Julie read the books and nodded during these conversations.

Finally they were on the case—prosecutors, defense lawyers, handlers, reporters, police, politicians, and community leaders. An official version of reality was constructed.

The dialogue and mythology of the Downtown Eastside didn't leave room for individuals. Everyone became a type or a figure. Activists and politicians talked about categories. The families and friends of the dead women worked hard to humanize their missing relatives, but then the families became a new kind of type. The etchings of grief made faces similar. It was a long process.

Judgment was clouded by assumptions and generalizations.

During the trial and review, officials said they were sorry it had taken so long to arrest the serial killer. They were sorry they'd given these women less attention than they should have. They apologized in ways worded to limit liability.

"We need to do some soul-searching," they said, "and re-examine how we treat those most vulnerable in our society. How we view the vulnerable." But that's always what they say when things get bad. The city was a story of communities within communities. Power. Everyone came from somewhere. No one was self-made, including the mass murderer. The pattern is regularly ignored until it fills the frame. The state of emergency is not exception, but part of a larger rule.

The other story that overlapped this one without touching it was the preparation for the Olympics. Negotiations with teachers and transit workers and cops and firefighters were ongoing. Money flowed towards a new SkyTrain and the athletes' village.

Gentrification moved in fresh waves. A big glass digital clock was embedded beside the largest art gallery. In flashing blue it counted down the years, days, hours, minutes, seconds until the opening ceremony. The games were a man-made snow dream and the farmer was a monster hidden in plain white.

The Seattle free weekly published an in-depth essay about the pig farm. Julie met the journalist who wrote it at a birthday party. He was a cool drunk player who told his party audience details of their local story like it was a ghost tale. The well-mannered Canadian press reported on the story using lurid hints and asserting that it was being respectful. Canadians, Julie found, could not stop themselves from jabbing at their American counterparts even when they were failing themselves. The journalist was from Botswana and clearly considered this North American parsing absurd. He told the bleak Canadian story to the assembled gaggle of locals as a way of shaming, flirting with, and shocking. He had been to the crime scene and interviewed a forensic scientist working there.

"A charnel house," he said. "As bad as you can imagine. Worse. There were no whole bodies. The forensic team had to catalogue parts and smears and clothes and personal effects stored in freezers and buckets and drawers. They found severed hands and piles of bone. They found a dildo mounted on a handgun. He used the same tools he'd used on pigs. He fed those girls to pigs and then fed locals that meat. The stuff all mingled.

"What the hell is wrong with this place?" he asked, before shrugging with a laugh and pouring another drink.

38

The walls of Bad Manors studio smelled of mold mixed with soup.

When she started sleeping with a photographer, she realized the building's odor had seeped into her clothes and hair. Her sweater smells spoiled compared to his lavender detergent bedsheets.

She burned incense and stopped cooking onions or garlic, washed clothes and blankets often, and kept the windows open.

On clear days she would stare at the skateboarders doing tricks in the park, instead of looking at the applications, grade sheets, and Xeroxed articles on her desk.

Julie kept encountering the figure of the cutter; philosophers seemed to love these crazy girls. In *Welcome to the Desert of the Real*, Žižek used girl cutters as symbols of the dual human passions for semblance and the real. He saw cutters not as suicidal melancholics but as sensitive souls acting out against the virtualization of the environment. By cutting their bodies they were making desperate assertions that they were real physical beings and that reality existed and was important.

Though she read about it and vividly recalled Celine with blood running down her arms and Band-Aids under her dresses, she would not speak up in class. Julie hated the women in the Women's Studies classes who described their own experiences in relation to the text, but she remained silent about that as well. She hated the girl in her program who was writing a thesis on sex positivity. She made her face a mask. Julie actually preferred reading European men who clearly had female troubles.

Fading out of the class discussion about deserts as a shifting referent, she thought about the desert of her childhood. She got it—the theory—she thought. But what did this mean for real desert people?

Julie watched *The Passenger, Badlands, Zabriski Point, Paris, Texas*. These different deserts provoked the same feelings somehow. The more she read, the more she thought that for these artists the desert were not real places but voids to project into. The art house directors loved the landscape. To them it evoked death and spiritual rebirth. She imagined a German Marxist in dark glasses regarding White Sands, or a French deconstructionist rereading *Lolita* in a motel in Marfa. Ugh. The girl was not a girl, nor was the desert a desert. Desert people were as significant as rocks and lizards. All were backgrounds for alienated men and their beautiful women. Desert towns were for hiding. Motel mattresses squeaked and dipped into valleys. Heroes escaped in the dark without water. Villains and their demonic baby dolls got trashed beside fires. Pickup headlights beamed.

She love-hated the French theorist who wrote, "The Americans have no identity, but do have wonderful teeth." Still, she quoted him in essays.

Julie buckled down on her research, classwork, applications, and letters of inquiry, grade sheets, and meetings, in order to be considered smart by professors. She labored to get European theorists' subtle ideas. At parties she hoped the pretty PhDs mistook Value Village for Parisian designer. She aimed to be smart, thin, and appropriate, but always felt she could never quite escape the repulsing taint of trauma. Her research always twisted back towards the dark and gross as she kept trying to find something good within her abjection.

39

For a course Julie watched all of David Lynch's work. In one over-saturated week she consumed every episode of *Twin Peaks*. During the binge she thought of Donna Beth, who'd been obsessed with the show. It had been on TV during the run of *Peter Pan*, and she'd made her boyfriend record it on VHS when she was at rehearsals. Julie remembered hearing about it sidelong, but her parents hadn't watched it because they found it too disturbing.

It was at once funny and terrifying. Julie, like everyone, wanted to be Audrey, the bystander half-friend, the beautiful girl with the menacing father who escaped the traps and learned secret truths.

Laura was the horrifying spectre, monstrous victim twisting in the traps of her abuse. The ceiling fan spun when things were about to go bad. The image of a white fan spinning against a white ceiling was a visual motif. Laura let herself be murdered so she could escape. Bob possessed her father. Bob as her father raped her and she let herself go so she could escape, but she got caught in the black lodge.

From the TV, the man's voice cried in anguish, "Don't make me do this."

In season two the same bad things happened to Laura's cousin, who is played by the same actress, but with dark hair and glasses. Her body hurt the same.

"Don't make me do this."

Julie wrote that trauma attracts. Traumatized people are apt to catch one another in lifetime loops. In the show you can see Donna trying to understand Laura by studying the film of

Laura alive. Julie wrote and wrote but wasn't able to untangle Laura from Madeline, or Leland from Bob from Ben from Dale from mirror from mirror. She knew what happened even when she did not. The work was about trauma. Or it was not only about but rather reproduced the logic and texture of trauma. Sometimes the trauma is from deep heart hurt, or jealousy, or shame. Girl trauma. The girl who was raped by her father or her father's friend. Those possessed by Bob.

Episode after episode Julie sat in the dark with a blue and tan afghan over her pulled-up knees. People said the show was mysterious, but she felt she understood it. It was clear because the show mirrored experiences that were experiential shrapnel lodged in every girl, or at least all the ones Julie had ever known. Girls recognize girl trauma, and trauma doesn't tack rational.

After Donna Beth's murder the grown women had cried, whispering details among themselves but explaining to her and Celine only the general outline of crime. They'd tried to shelter them from the burden of intimate horror. They told a story of a murder with only a little blood; a murder with a memorial scholarship and bouquets at the end of it.

40.

In the summer she went to New Mexico to visit her parents. They said come for a while, you haven't been back in so long, so she booked a three-week trip. After three days her father ran out of things to discuss, so he took to telling the plot of his favorite HBO show. Her mother encouraged her to relax, offered to drive her to the university pool even though it was walking distance. Julie felt fourteen again, except this time she had credit cards and debt and a worry crease between her eyes. Her mother asked if she needed to see an optometrist.

Afternoons unfolded slow motion. She decided to join Facebook and friended all her Vancouver and Portland friends. They appeared in a row of tiny photos. They appeared in a scroll of playful to-be statements. There was her best Vancouver friend with a profile picture of him hugging a husky puppy with bright-blue eyes. Ayden is in the lost and found, please come claim him. That annoying guy from class Jay is looking for a new bike. Clara, the girl she knew from her Portland French class, is writing it in diamond, bitches.

She found Celine and requested her friendship. Her request was accepted. Her most recent status said Celine is saying it with flowers.

Julie went deep into her friend's many pictures, piecing together journeys across Europe. Recent photos clearly charted a relationship with a blond guy. There were pictures of the man making a face on the back of a bike with a city skyline behind. There was a picture of Celine—who still had similar hair and fashion sense to that of her teen years—pressed close to the guy. His fingers made a heart. The caption read, Engaged! C+B 4ever, followed by many messages of congratulations. You guys! How incredible!

It hurt Julie somehow that she hadn't known, even though she'd neglected communication as much as Celine had.

In another photo Julie recognized the background as White Sands National Monument. It had been a magic, spacey destination for many of her teenage drives.

In the picture Celine wore a blue scarf and a half-smile. The luminescent sand formed a bluish background behind her that echoed the sky's hue. A thin band of pink-purple-yellow mountain clouds made the horizon line. Celine looked straight into the camera and beyond it to the man—it had to be him taking it—adoringly. Julie had seen that look before. A Celine face classique. With a little pang Julie felt like a voyeur. Of course, people keep living without you. She felt silly as she wrote the note.

41.

Dearest Celine,

It's been so long. I don't even know where you are.

I'm in New Mexico. It's August, I came to see my parents and to have some time to research my thesis, but it's a million degrees and my parents don't know what to do with me. So I've been walking to the university library, then to the one coffee shop, then back to the library. Stepping from over-air-conditioned to furnace blast to over-air-conditioned makes me sick. I carry a cardigan to put over my tank top. I saw that guy Jeff waiting tables at La Posta. He's fat now. Do you remember him? He was Miguel's friend. I remember we thought he was so cute. But now. Ugh. I pretended I didn't see him.

Being here reminds me of you, but also of all the reasons we left. God.

I drink the weak coffee, read without absorbing, avoid writing, or planning, or problem-solving. But overall I'm in a fine mood. I don't let things bother me. Quail coo rhythmically outside my childhood window. When they cry out it means all is well. When they go silent you know danger is near. All is well. All is well.

Where are you? This weird system says you are in Chicago. True? How are you doing? Who is your handsome man? You are engaged?! I wish we could talk, you have so much news! I, on the other hand, am just an overgrown, perpetual student. Someday I swear I'll learn.

Miss you, my friend—

xo

Julie

42.

She left her parents' August desert swelter early. On airport TV, CNN played silent. The closed captioning made the story come out like a jerky poem.

Why did this
promising young football
player kill
his wife and child?

The anchor wondered if brain injuries could have been a factor.

At Canadian customs she had to renew her student visa for one more year.

"Anything to declare?" asked the thick officer.

Her friend Ayden had offered to pick her up. They'd been getting close before she left and she felt so happy to see him parked in the pick-up zone. He was house-sitting for a teacher and had the use of her Volvo. When she came through the sliding glass doors he was busy telling a guard she would be there momentarily.

"You can't park here. You have to move now or I will ticket you sir."

"See!" He gestured at Julie. "We were just leaving."

"Sir asshole," he said just inside the car.

There was a post-rain sunset, with just a few fine slices of flame showing through the baroque cloudscape of rose and slate. It felt like she'd jumped more than location. This was a different universe. Late August on the border was nowhere near late August in the Pacific Northwest. Duh, but still.

The trees made an inky green-black smear through the damp windshield. On a downtown corner a group of girls teetered in velour and platforms, waving their hands frantic for a cab.

"Sometimes," Ayden mumbled, "the waxed smoothness of this city really . . . It just . . . This place is a horror story."

"I missed you my friend!" Julie laughed, squeezing his shoulder.

43.

A new semester started. Julie was committed to being healthier and less obsessive, so she signed up for a yoga membership at one of the many studios in the city.

She'd been practicing on and off since Portland and found the studios comforting. Studios everywhere seemed to share one vibe. There seemed to be aesthetic rules, unlike her chaotic home. Wood floor and altars draped in saris, practice rooms cleared with sage and incense, watercoolers and shoe cubbies.

Earnest and kind teachers with nice hands and effortless handstands liked to speak about moving past anger and suffering. They touched their students gently. They spoke of emotions as if they were just storms, never mentioning concrete brutality. At the latest studio, classes began with stories. One time the teacher described how she'd broken free of her PR career in order to follow a spiritual path.

Julie loved these people and places guiltily. Her academic inclination branded them decontextualized temples for yuppie solipsism. But she kept coming back.

In class she fell into breath just as the teachers instructed. Just turn off your thoughts. All those Lululemon asses. She didn't care. She needed it for all the sick anger that pervaded her body. After classes she'd feel floaty and smooth.

At school the workload was immediately too much. The wrinkle between her eyebrows got deeper.

She watched online footage of mass protests around a free trade summit. Though they were from Canada, the shots could be from any downtown in any major city. Security forces had erected temporary twenty-foot-high fences around office towers. Thousands of protesters had taken to the streets, a handful of them black-clad anarchists. The news showed the anarchists because smashing bottles and burning police cars made a compelling spectacle. The same car burned in a loop. It only took one window to frame a conversation. "Look at these people!" officials howled. The police charged chanting groups and made six hundred arrests.

She imagined the artificially cooled conference rooms where world leaders discussed Third World debt. Julie did not make this up. The stories were out there, events occurred. That was not in question.

At school she was sometimes criticized for her scattered methods. Teachers either loved or hated how her wavy parallel lines never clearly crossed but often kissed. She was working on her theory. Small parts came into focus then shimmered away. Ideas looped back like snakes eating their own tails. "Just the tip," Julie whispered to herself.

She got a little nothing message from Celine that outlined a happy life of art and love in the Midwest. They traded a few jokes about the desert and spoke vaguely of hanging out if they both ended up there for Christmas. September was unseasonably cold. The burn of car door handles and motionless desert afternoons seemed like hallucinations. People move on, she told herself.

She closed her computer, laid her hands on her desk, her head on her hands. She refused to name those she missed. It was all too much.

She often got headaches from the school's fluorescent lights, but still she strained to speak articulately in class. She felt so close to understanding, to finding answers. Sometimes though, she felt like what her professors were doing was rearranging questions so they appeared to be answers. She wanted to untangle the most complicated knots. She vibrated.

She was to submit her thesis in three days.

Over the phone, her mom advised, "Leave the house, take a break."

At the Italian café the TVs were showing soccer; they always showed soccer.

In her book she read, "In the good labyrinth there appears to be order. There is the illusion of some logic and calm—however within that there is the madness of slight variation. Things seem to fall back on themselves or in on the wanderer."

44

Julie traveled uphill to the main campus to see a visiting scholar speak on bodies. Hers felt achy and puffy. As the bus made its slow assent she composed a list: more yoga, less drinking. School's countdown was culminating in a spiral of stress and compulsions. She bit all her nails, didn't eat. Outside the bus windows all the surfaces were coated with a day's and a night's and a day's worth of rain.

Her school had various conference rooms and auditoriums, all with the same industrial carpets and metal chairs with jewel-toned cushions. Each room was named after a company that had given money to the school. Her course on the cyborg had been held in a room named for a subsidiary of Anheuser-Busch. The class on the Frankfurt School convened in a room named for a gold-mining conglomerate.

The visiting scholar was highly regarded for his work on German literature. Bald and slight, his head and neck framed by white collar gave him the look of a Dutch portrait subject. His dark sweater disappeared into the auditorium curtains. He spoke carefully. As is the style of academic lecturers, he established a ground from which the talk would grow. Researching was a form of tilling. But the rocks were good, as were the roots. Maybe he was not a gardener, but an archeologist. Maybe he was not an archeologist, but a builder. Maybe not a builder, but an architect of impossible bridges. The careful man stated that he was not an art historian, but wished to start with a painting.

He put David's *Death of Marat* up on the screen. Marat was dead in his bathtub, the space above his figure dark and heavy. The scholar suggested that the black space, prefiguring

Malevich's black square, was an abstract stand-in for the unrepresentable people of the democracy Marat fought for, the revolutionary subjects of a new modern system.

The scholar argued that in a monarchy the king's body doubled; he was both a real person and a physical embodiment of the state, having therefore to bear the health and sickness of the whole. In some way, pre-democratic people were not forced to bear the health of their law—it was divine right that the king's body had to bear.

But things were different now. In a democracy, individuals can't get a piece of the action without becoming sick with poisons of nationhood. Democracy offers everyone a spoonful of the oily poison of the state. We are all just a little responsible for the violence our leaders oversee, Julie scribbled.

Marat was a doctor afflicted with a terrible skin condition. When revolution shattered the body of the king, the illnesses it carried broke up into as many shards as there were people—each person got one. Then we all became infected.

He said these artworks—David's and Malevich's—could be viewed as part of a continuum of art history, revolution, and the modern project. They were like windows "through which the revolutionary spirits of radical destruction could enter the space of culture and reduce it to ashes."

His voice strained into the auditorium full of silent, serious professors, PhD students, various and sundry. He continued. Freud was significant partly because he recognized that mental and physical symptoms developed in parallel to the spread of modern democracy.

Julie tried and failed to write down whole quotes, but in the end scrawled scraps.

He quoted and referenced. The people in the auditorium, classmates and teachers, trafficked in this material. They refined, packaged, traded, cut, and consumed these kinds of ideas.

On the screen behind the scholar played a video of a white horse dropped with a shot in the head from a bolt gun. Then he played the early Edison film of an elephant being electrocuted with metal sandals. Her body produced so much smoke it filled the shot and hid her death. After that he showed a clip of soldiers torturing a main character by tying a wasp's nest to his face.

"I'll now open this up for questions."

Julie's hand lay on a white notebook paper covered with words scribbled fast. The auditorium curtain undulated as she unfocused. She felt the familiar intoxication of complex thinking, the dangerous allure of a mind high.

45.

It was the day Saddam Hussein was hanged. Julie listened to the news as she put on her yoga clothes.

At the studio desk one of the bevy of pretty girls, in a cardigan and flush with the heat of too much Ashtanga, signed her in. They smiled at one another.

Inside the practice room the teacher instructed Julie, a dozen other women, and the one man to close their eyes and chant peace in a language none of them really knew.

After a few minutes of silent meditation the teacher began to read them a story.

"There once was a woman. She was a most terrible terrorist." Julie wondered if this story came randomly from a book the teacher had to read from or if she'd chosen it specially. "Outwardly she appeared to be a mystic with great power.

"However, performing mystic processes does not necessarily purify one's heart.

"One day she came in contact with Krishna. When she came in contact with him he began to drain her body. For him it was effortless, but for her it was painful, terrifying. She could feel the very life coming out. She was struck with fear and then suffered terrible pain; trying to resist by all means the process of purification.

"Now when we think of Krishna, we must remember he is all attractive, all auspicious. He is above the dualities. Transcendental in every respect. Therefore whatever comes in contact with him becomes auspicious and attracted to him. Like the sun he purifies all that he touches.

"The poison within her heart started coming out. All poisons came out—all lust, envy, greed, all pride, and all illusion so deeply stored in her mind began pouring out. My God, how painful!

"As this was happening Krishna was gracefully dancing. Every time his foot touched her it felt like a thunderbolt crushing her skull. All her karma came out. This is the process of purification. It's an ugly matter to see inside.

"Brilliant flames arose from her body. At first they burned bright, but over time they were less and less until they were extinguished. All that was left was terrible, black poison. What was left of her understood that everything was about to be finished. She thought: I am this body, I loved to kill, I loved to cause sorrow in the hearts of others, and I loved to control people. But now all that is over.

"Krishna danced over her until she died, actually died. She fell dead. Her body was gigantic. You can imagine how big she was and terrible.

"The cowherders asked, 'How could we live with such an enormous form taking up so much of the pasturelands? Where will the cows eat grasses?' So they chopped up her body and lit her on fire, and as they were burning, a miracle took place. The fragrance coming from her body was nectar, sweet as the most ambrosial incense. Upon smelling the fragrance of the smoke emanating from her burning body many inhabitants were astonished.

"But through this death she attained life because all her illusion died within her. That ego was all she knew. In her death she was granted her eternal life in the spiritual world. Krishna had killed her false ego and in the process he awakened the core of her heart where the soul resides. She had been cleansed. Even the body left behind was purified. She was liberated."

The sky was a brilliant, fresh-washed blue that was shifting in its cloud-massed edges to ultramarine, to cerulean. Julie remembered reading somewhere the word blue related to an ancient word *blao*, which meant 'shining.' The book said that ancient people didn't distinguish the color blue. The sky blazed with the first blush of sunset. She wanted to be liberated from her evil shit like the bad lady. Though enlightenment seemed pretty impossible this go-round, she thought she could at least burn away that week's frozen tension from her shoulders. Baby steps, she told herself, as the lithe teacher instructed everyone in a low voice to "please stand and bring your hands into prayer position."

Julie reached up to wipe her tears away. Breathe. It will be okay. Just keep going.

On the bus back home after class she tried thinking against closed eyelids, but three guys across from her were laughing their heads off and taking cell phone photos. One kicked her foot with a purpose she ignored.

For dinner she had a handful of frozen blueberries, chocolate, and a big glass of whiskey.

A little sloshed she walked to the skate park, hoping to see the handsome teenagers gliding around like it was nothing, but none were out. Too late. In their place a jogger hustled past with high-tech gear striped with reflective panels. A sketch of his body shown as he moved away from her. The streetlights went on. By chance it wasn't raining. This was the closest she'd ever come to what she didn't know. It got darker and darker.

3.

Flowers in the Addict

46.

In their home country, in another reality, Celine became a lover. She'd always wanted to be one, rehearsing the part year after year with different men until she finally met one who wanted the full performance. Brendan wondered if she could come visit. She played coy. "How funny. I was hoping you'd ask."

His adopted home of Chicago spread flat, bound on one side by a great lake that ruffled around its edges. She saw it first from the air, which doomed her to romanticize. Through the plane window she saw the sun's rays painting diagonal lines through holey clouds down to the lake where they bounced back into black and silver glass. She saw a model city arranged against baroque skyscape.

The flatness of the landscape had been a dream for modernism's makers. They had bisected their creation with angled streets that all ran to and away from the encircled center. Everything was made flat and quilt-like by the plane perspective.

Her view of the Loop gave way to the neighborhoods of browns and greens, concrete and brick interrupted by little yards and larger parks. Finally she landed and found Brendan on the other side of security, waiting to take her into the city.

Before her visit their trail of text messages and emails had grown long, tracing countless intimate lifelines. They traded opinions and tales about childhoods, deserts versus woods, collages and photographs, and brushes with the law. They skimmed the Internet for jokes to make the other laugh.

"A Freudian slip is where you say one thing, but you mean your mother," she offered.

"What's the difference between an Irish funeral and an Irish wedding?" he wrote back.

"What?"

"One less drunk."

At once her emotional life changed and the idea of not knowing Brendan seemed terrible. He had not been there, and then he was, dwelling in her mind. She visited him three times in two months. He came to see her in New York once. She studied his marks of stability: an apartment, school, a job, and a cat. When they were together whatever they did became special. They were never tired, even when asleep. Only in the process of falling in love with him did she realize she'd never done it before. And what shocked her more was that he also wanted to be with her.

During their visits they played house. Made the bed. Worked during the day. For dinner they cooked eggplant parmesan, borscht. They would have salads and bread and wine and glasses of beer. Small squares of chocolate with whiskey. While he rolled a joint she would make espressos so they could be up as they walked through the empty streets of his neighborhood.

"Hippie speedball," he joked.

At the end of her third visit to Chicago he said, "Maybe this is impulsive, crazy even, but maybe you should move here. If you want."

She could not believe her good luck. It was mystical. She had been looking for this lover for forever without realizing. She gave her roommate notice. Within the month she'd departed and arrived.

Brendan reminded Celine of boys from her teen years, but he also mystified her. Though she hadn't met anyone like him, she'd crushed on boys just like him. He was so familiar yet she didn't understand him. A man with the kind of face that attracts police attention, he said with a smirk that would make somebody want to slap him. She kissed instead. Like no one else, and karmically summoned. This was the spell they told one another.

She was giddy as he cooked dinner for her first night living with him. They talked poetry and friends.

Outside, some drunk men's voices echoed against the buildings. A clatter announced bikes falling over. More yelling. A breeze blew in and a moment later so did a brown bird. It came as an explosion of wildlife in a regular domestic scene. What surprised them was how something so adept at dodging obstacles outside immediately began to knock against everything—ceiling, fridge, cabinet, walls—with all its tiny force. She feared it was going to break its own neck.

"Open the window!"

"It is already."

"Then wider."

"Whatever you say dear."

"Don't scare him."

"Okay. Settle down. Let's all breathe. Bird, breathe."

"Okay. Let's turn off the lights."

"Why?"

"Maybe it will calm him down?" She laughed.

"He's panicking from all the light pollution."

"So sad, little buddy." They turned off the lights and the bird became a smudge against the wall above the cabinet, regarding them with tiny shining eye dots.

"Maybe it would like to live here."

"If I were him, I would," she said. After waving dish towels towards the windows for a while, they sat down on the floor and lit cigarettes.

"You'd better go, you little thing, before we change our minds and keep you here. You'll die from all the love."

The bird found the window and flew away. They left the lights off for the rest of the night.

47.

Sleep-deprived from drink, infatuation, and sex, they stumbled around her new unfamiliar city, his city. Each neighborhood appeared cinematic because each one mimicked other neighborhoods in other countries she'd visited. The surroundings made her insides hum because they stirred memories of elsewhere. Fragments of the world made mosaics of the streets. From the beginning Brendan spoke the lover's dialect of imagery and suggestion. He unwrapped his crumbly city as if it were a Spanish cookie or a Mexican candy. Every walk they took was a treat he gave for her special worthiness.

"That's the junkie bridge and the next one is where people

go for cocaine." The structure he pointed to looked workaday Midwestern. Office workers and tourists rushed and strolled.

"How can you tell?"

"You have to realize drugs flow under most of reality."

"There's the museum. We'll go sometime, but for now forget about it. Just the trash heaps of dead pillagers anyhow. Instead let's go home, get high, and then I want to take your clothes off." She walked faster, smiling. She put her hands together. Here is the church and here is the steeple, open the doors, where are the people?

They went out and out and out. He smiled and danced drunk. She held his hand as they kept dancing. The people of the city were changed by her mood; they appeared more beautiful, happier, and more free. They laughed amid radio hits and fragrant steam. The bartender started singing along to Lil Wayne.

Then they were in his apartment that was all of a sudden hers too. The tree outside tapped the window. Plants in ceramic pots. Framed photos. Keys on a hook. He talked like he'd been waiting for forever for her ears. He said darling and sweetheart and then there was the way he laughed with his whole self. His gray cat appeared and disappeared. Brendan opened the window to allow cool air to slink in.

"I think I'm totally in love with you," she said, then felt a stabbing in her side.

"Be careful with that. I'm bad news," he replied like it was funny. But then she pouted so he wrapped her in kisses and babies and darlings.

48.

So. Two as one all at once. Maybe it was too much or too hard, but she could not convince herself to go another way. While thinking of him, riding her new bike, Celine turned onto a bridge. It was sometime during the long twilight of July. She saw a burst of citizen-sparked fireworks over the Southside. It was Independence Day in the United States of America.

She could fly past anything now, she thought. She would be okay. It was a holiday night, absurdly hot. She slipped by a shirtless man yelling obscenities, through an intersection, passed children shooting bottle rockets, people playing softball under hard lights, graffitied retaining walls, rose bushes littering the sidewalk with pink and brown confetti. She wore a white shirt, black shorts, white bra and panties, navy sneakers, and no socks. She felt wonderful.

The saturated colors pulsed before her slightly blurred vision. There were murals on the subjects of immigration and the pain of colonization. People had painted doorways golden and balconies with cobalt and caramel trims. She locked her bike on a pole beneath an anti-gentrification poster.

In the grocery store, rust stucco and pineapple-hued walls made everyone cinematic. But then again, maybe it was the heat or the love or the pot. How could she untangle such sensations? They needed watermelon and seltzer, chips and avocados.

"I think I've been here before."

49.

Each day after her love went to work Celine stayed alone in their crumbly apartment with the wonderful light. The place was on the end of a street with uninterrupted views of a military-minded high school. Every weekday morning, while she made coffee with cinnamon, the sweat-suited teens chanted in the yard. Some afternoons too, when she was being bad and leaning out the window to exhale joint smoke, and the kids were there again with their echoey shouts as they played after-school soccer. The kids were almost all Mexican-American as far as she could tell, and the school itself was named after the famous general Benito Juárez.

The Pilsen neighborhood had been built up in waves. Germans and Irish and Czechs until many Mexican families, displaced by destruction elsewhere, began moving in. Because of the city's structural racism, the Europeans there moved north, and it became the biggest Mexican community in the city. The buildings had a kind of Bavarian style. Celine loved the contrast—buildings designed like cuckoo clocks filled with Veracruz beach posters, taquerías and tortilleria and Tejano music. Catholicism shot through everything. Basing her opinions mostly on her own angry Irish relatives, Celine liked to say she preferred Mexican Catholicism. She enjoyed hyperbole and adopting arbitrary opinions. Brendan pointed this out as a flaw: Pilsen felt like a familiar warm community embedded within a strange, cold land.

Each morning she would walk to where a bus would come every twenty minutes. Her route passed the Juárez Driving School, a big lot of semis bordering train tracks and an empty lot of feathery weeds and random piles of gravel.

The Loop's glossy buildings stood sentinel in the distance, the castle of city power appearing much farther than it was in reality.

50

In the drafty kitchen, standing above the flickering burner, Brendan instructed, "Breathe in and hold it for a long time." The gray cat wound his way round bike tires.

The smoke was hotter and more acrid than she imagined it would be. Painful coughing turned into laughing, a whiff of singed something rode along a draft of grass through the open window. Her brain felt like a balled-up wet scarf. It was raining after all. But then somehow her face was wrapped in the scarf. She followed her breath out the room. To extract self from self proved difficult. Her love put a scalding cup of tea in her hand. She found herself flapping on the green velvet chair. No, that's the ghost-white curtain. If only she could get around front and see the whole picture. Eyes on her green skirt and blue velvet pillow. We are human. We are going to die someday. There's a hand on the pillow, or a model of a hand, my hand. Very convincing.

"My self-medicating has to do with anxiety." He laughed, throwing his voice.

"Let's go out," he said. He always said that.

Celine and Brendan crossed the threshold between dripping pungent night and dark-wood bar. It smelled like smokers wearing sweaters, sweating. The foody and damp air hit her in a wave. Bodies so close she could feel little springs of wool in the back of her throat. Perhaps if she hadn't taken those drugs. Duck and cover, her body said with every twitch. There was a conversation. They were in it. It went something like this.

"They say when the wall fell, East German police burst the huge office furnace, stuffing it with incriminating documents.

Men in charge disappeared into mobs on the street. Half the population had spied on the other half. Many spies got away with their violence because all the paper and guilt got muddled in the heap. A mess of statue parts and sledge-hammered walls."

"Right. I mean it's crazy. I mean, you can't throw half the population in jail, can you?"

"Can't you?"

51.

Celine and Brendan spent two years together. She felt always on-notice. As if the love she offered him was forever verging on not enough. More was not enough. She frustrated him. He was frustrated by her. She didn't even know how to give enough. She didn't even know. He asked for a lot. Troubles at work and obscure rages at friends and family. He broke with their social group. She defended him and justified the fights. She tried to mold herself into his ideal sounding board and defender. Somehow it always got turned around. When she would rage at him, he would appear satisfied. "That's how you really are, not as sweet as you pretend to be," he said. She got confused. She was a selfish whore without realizing it.

She discovered new hollow spaces within herself. She gave space and also tried to hold the space. They got engaged when he gave her a jagged silver ring designed after that Joy Division cover. Love will tear us apart. It was silly and deeply felt. Emotion and poetry. She gave him a signet ring and a book about Félix González-Torres inscribed, "To my perfect lover."

It did not go well. She was living in his city, amongst the friends he kept. Out of her depth, as they say. Difficulties arose.

Roses tattooed. Whiskey soured. Coke appeared and vanished in lines on the glass of a picture taken down from the wall. Still she believed.

At the bar she pleaded, "Let's go home, it's late. Tomorrow we can get up early and have a healthy day." He ordered another and she did too, giving in, enabling, he'd say. Probably true.

"Don't be such a hater," he'd say.

"Let's stay out a little later and have some fun."

52.

Their little balcony door was open to catch the breeze. Though the sun had long since set, the heat was still pressing down on everything, making Celine feel slow motion.

Down on the opposite side of the street a group of men were smoking and laughing outside a bar. Yellow lights from the apartments made the scene cinematic against the weird purple of the sky above. The strange hues of a Midwestern night maybe on the verge of a thunderstorm. Through other open windows came the sounds of radio news, plate clatter, Top 40, and unintelligible conversations. Maybe it wouldn't rain. Their white and blue curtain billowed out.

Brendan came up with a freshly rolled joint held in a soft pinch. "You want some?" She did.

Celine inhaled. They passed it back and forth while watching the street. Brendan took a last inhale, then flicked the stub, its still-glowing tip flying in an arc to the asphalt.

They were flying to New York. He would visit family while she went to see a friend up in Montréal. It would be the longest time apart since they'd met. He was the most hurtful and the tenderest man she'd ever been with. It was too much and not enough. Their love persisted far beyond too much. Whatever was her had blurred. Whatever.

From down the block two small cars turned, driving much faster than was normal. It was a dead end. The driver of the first car went as far as the cement block at the end of the street before three men threw open the doors. They ran in different directions. Brendan crouched; Celine followed him to her knees. The men outside the bar had disappeared. Across from them someone slid closed their window with a click. A second car appeared. Two went down the alley. The first car was a smudge on the dark street. Barking punctuated the quiet. A man emerged from the bar. Brendan reached for Celine's shoulder. The young man had something in his hand. For a moment all the men huddled next to a gray car door. Their hands were moving. Then from the car came a hiss. Then the car was on fire. The men disappeared. After some uncountable minutes, the door of the bar opened and the sound of Whitney Houston's voice came out hazy. Each word breaking over the next.

"Should we call the cops?"

"No."

53.

The curtains, now drawn over the glass door, moved, or maybe they weren't moving, but Celine's eyes were playing tricks. Somehow the blue flowers on the white background were not staying still.

She and Brendan sat in silence.

He put his hand on the nape of her neck. He pet down from neck to shoulder to breasts to jeans' button then tugged. Celine moved according to mental pictures of how she should appear.

Be a pretty girl with back arched and underwear matched. She thought of the car outside on fire. His dick half-soft in her mouth felt vulnerable, but after a few minutes she was choking.

The shaved back of his head made a very faint friction noise against the sofa corduroy. He held a fistful of her hair and kept her face bumping against his crotch longer than she had ever done before. She gulped air when he pulled her head back. Loss and gain are brothers twain. He slapped her lightly and pulled her up.

"Touch yourself."

As he stumbled on his jeans in a rush to the bedroom she held her body tentatively. Where was she? The bow of her bra comforted her. Coming back he took her shoulders and turned them away. He pushed her open. His fingers felt for a second clumsy and foreign, but their insistence made her wet still. She lost the outside.

"What do you want?" A vacuum formed, pulling air and light.

"What do you want?" His thighs slapped her at a steady beat. She realized she had drooled on a cushion.

"What do you want? Tell me slut. Do as you're told."

She turned her face into the cushion to block out everything but an interior pulse. She blurred. Lights traveled across the curtains.

"I want you to hurt me."

He groaned a little satisfied. "I know you do. I have to. I have to."

She knew nothing of this person but how his shirts and come smelled, how his mole and tattoo aligned, how he put cinnamon in the coffee, and how he spit off the balcony after smoking.

Once they'd finished she curled up against him. The light caught his thick eyelashes in profile. They beat the air like insect wings. She felt very tender.

54.

Dearest darling Brendan,

Whenever we are apart all I want to do is talk to you, with you, tell you about what I'm seeing and thinking.

It's 2:34 a.m., humid hot. I rode my bike over the dark but somehow bright, potholed streets. All day I've been having an internal conversation broken by moments of actual conversation, about . . . about how I have so long felt you are my psychic twin, about how the trust or lack of trust in oneself plays against the trust in another person. How can I trust you if I can't trust myself? Or rather, more importantly, how can I learn to trust myself so I can earn back your trust?

The third stop on the train between NYC and Montréal is Hudson. The train traces the river bank we were on when we visited your mom not so long ago, distant cliffs and close woods. For much of the ride it's as if the train is moving directly over water, it's all you can see out the windows. I was passing through the landscape of your youth on my way to a place I associate so much with my own becoming. I carry you around in my mind like it's a pocket.

I saw Erin's dance piece. *Wolves and Selves* was the title. At the end of the piece her partner, who has laid down naked, gets back up with shreds of brown fur stuck to her body. Raising the wolf of your dead child self. She bears her teeth. They at times grab one another's faces, push one another's arms, violently but without anger.

After the show we met up with people we knew ten years ago. They looked the same but older. We all sat around talking, seated at the same table but in different universes in a sweltering back patio beneath old trees.

We talked about spirits as in ghosts and as in alcohol. Medicine as poison or potions. Erin smoked Fantasia Nat Sherman's. She gave me a blue one while she had yellow. You should have been there. I looked for you. You would have liked our conversation of loops and free associations. She understands, in a way few of my friends can, my sense of you and I, I and I.

Back where I was staying, after writing the first part of this note, I padded between the bathroom and the bed, naked in the dark, too hot to sleep, too late to be anything but silent. My glasses were steaming up even. I thought about sex and its potential for transformation. To trust someone to fuck you.

The density of our relating astonishes me. I have to imagine (at least at this moment tonight) that we are giving birth not to the end of our love, but letting it rise up again in a new form.

I only hope you want to read this.

With the lightest and the heaviest heart,

Love,

C

55.

At art school people liked talking about 'the other.' The phrase always had aural italics—*the Other.* It carried weight. Celine found herself doing it, but felt dumb sometimes—often—as the premise of this Self/Other seemed to arise from mad, old, emotionally isolated European men.

From what she could tell many people felt radical talking about a blurring of Self and Other, whereas she felt like nothing but an ill-defined part of an amorphous whole. Crying was as contagious as laughter. But then, of course, these epic individuals she read so much about were so defined by what they were not. They were not women, not emotional, not mystical, not native, not children.

Rational, masculine, white, European, gay or straight, but oh so rational and reasonable. On the one hand, everyone at art school was rolling their collective eyes, but still these guys were haunting everyone's conversation. They were the rocks everyone else's watery whateverness had to flow around.

And then there were their rebellious sons writing as if it were radical. What if we were in fact being touched as we touched? How wild! What if dreams and intuitions and smoke-filled rituals did have significance, they posited. No, she mocked in the margins. What if! All these other brilliant people got caught up in protesting, in asserting they too were actually people, and what it meant to be a person did not hinge on singular precious subjectivity. It did not hinge on sons throwing a grown-up, intellectual tantrum about how they were not, not, not like their mothers.

She got so angry. It was addictive. She wasn't sure why it made her so angry—some kind of resentment, a perverse desire to burst the casual comfort of all these east coast and Midwestern artists. The edges were so far. She longed for something cutting. But then, perhaps that was just her old way of defining herself.

56

The art Celine was making wasn't being well received, but she couldn't stop or make it more likeable. For a while she turned her pictures to face the wall.

She collected images from the Internet and arranged them beside her own snapshots. In one photo a man lay on cracked dirt, his head turned. Behind the man was a line of legs, cut off above the knees. They appeared to belong to men and women in flip-flops or sneakers, one barefoot, another set of legs beside a bicycle wheel. The newspaper caption said the lying man was a message for the neighborhood. His wrists were handcuffed together in front. A rag protruded from his open mouth. Though there were probably many more outside the frame, there were at least fifty visible knives stabbed in him. This excess was the cartel's form of communicating with those standing, the still living.

The photo was taken so close to her hometown. Taken where she, Julie, and Miguel used to party. This photo was taken in someone's hometown. It struck her dumb.

She began collecting blankets from Salvation Armies and Thrift Towns. A cheap navy micro-fleece printed with moon and stars; another one, dusty-rose covered with grandmotherly arabesques; a large one with a black background and a pack of wolves gathered around a large, central wolf throwing its head back in iconic howl. Howling.

They were the same kind of blankets people sold at flea markets and in empty lots in the desert from the back of pickup trucks. They were the same kind she saw in photos of people murdered in the Drug War. In the photos, it seemed as though regular people had draped the blankets, not medics or police. Celine wondered where they came from. Had they come straight off people's beds? Because of them, the desert, the spot where these bodies were dumped or where these people died became like bedrooms. Or maybe for the still living there was the need to domesticate and comfort, to re-privatize the shame and horror publicly acted out.

Against her studio's white walls she hung the blankets like flags or curtains. Another day she took them down and lay beneath them. She lay beneath them still.

In a class crit she sat around with other students as their teacher riffed on the history of textiles in performance.

57.

An hour into one particularly brutal argument, Brendan told her, "You need to get the fuck out." It was his home, he said.

"But I came here for you. You wanted me here."

"Ultimately you chose, knowing the risks. I warned you. We both have to be free to change our minds."

"Why are you so cruel?" she screamed.

He could turn, and she found she could too. She thought of the viciousness her mother described passing between her grandparents. She felt compassion and pain. Now I know what happens in fights of love, she thought. She thought they were arguing to stay within the magic bubble their love created, but she found herself defending its very existence. She crumpled and walked out with just coat and keys.

It was freezing. Leafless trees crosshatched the city park. It was a setting for an expressionist drama, a charcoal drawing. A huge machine drove by flinging salt. Every step in her inappropriate shoes offered a new opportunity to fall on the brittle, salty, grimed-up ice sidewalk. Car exhaust coated the road's crusted edges. At this time only a few hardcore winter joggers were out, singing along to the thrum of their own endorphins.

Laboring through collapsing snow ripples, Celine mentally re-performed both parts of their fight scene in an effort to reach a happy resolution. She was crying and practicing the speech where she said she understood Brendan's fears and wanted to repair the harm she'd caused. Singing is good for the heart and lungs, said her Chinese doctor. She sang to herself, "You are protected by a white light, your love is protected by a white light." Snot coated her sleeve.

Stumbling means getting not just wet but filthy. Frustrated breath condensed on her collar. Happy Year of the Dragon, or was it the Snake? Her acupuncturist said which, but she forgot. She had a hard time breathing, which had to do with all the fear living in her lungs.

58.

After they'd made up, Celine and Brendan agreed some space would be healthy. She took a Greyhound north to visit Erin in Toronto. Erin got her up early for yoga classes. Afterward they'd drink smoothies and read in coffee shops. They looked at art and Erin introduced Celine to some of her sweet, creative friends. Three weeks passed like this. Celine wrote Brendan many long emails trying to express some new hope and calm.

It was a mild, early spring afternoon. Erin took Celine by ferry to an island where there was going to be a party. The island had a closed amusement park, many geese, and no cars. They took mushrooms, and as the hallucinogens took effect they lay in the baby grass marveling at birdsong and some people playing tennis. They walked around the island taking photos of one another and random details—plastic swan planters in front of one house and a brick walkway glowing rust beside purple and yellow crocuses. The sun blazed down and disappeared. At the party it was cold again, but there was a fire that mesmerized. Behind the fire the downtown lights shone and bounced against the black lake water. Celine thought this was a turning point, turning her towards a happier period.

On the cramped maroon bus seat Celine typed a letter to Brendan on her phone. Once the bus crossed the border, she sent the message. She was carrying with her more positive and supportive love. She was bringing clean energy into their bubble. She thought that if she could write a letter that was a true reflection of her heart, she could redeem and recover the swoony bond they'd had.

59.

Dear love,

Last night Erin and I talked about our beloved dead friend and lightning in the desert.

If you and I can be free with each other again, I would like to take you to the desert in the summer, when it's common to see lightning every night. Sometimes during the day you can see it rain without the rain ever hitting the ground, what's called verga. I used that word in an essay once and my teacher criticized my use of it. He called it ostentatious. But how else can I describe the rain that hovers between fall and evaporation?

You can see great distances in all directions in the desert; you can see lights a hundred miles away.

In the desert we could go to Carlsbad Caverns. At the natural entrance bats fly out very fast at sunset. At the opposite end of the cave system you can take an elevator right down to a snack bar that incorporates stalagmites and stalactites into its architecture. It's an oven on the surface in summer, but a constant temperature underground all year round.

When I was sixteen I had both my first kiss and gave my first blow job. In too-quick succession, a matter of months. I gave or rather had a college guy's cock given to me when we were in his car, parked in the desert. He pushed my head down all the way until I gagged, but I trusted he wasn't trying to hurt me. He had the same name as you, no lie.

I remember how strange this was, going and feeling pushed towards the point of arrival/departure. Come in my throat. Someone pushing me to be good at an action I didn't know the contours of. When I/he finished, we saw lightning a long way off. This too is true. He told me my way reminded him of the flowers in the garden of the house he lived in when he was a young kid. He told me at another time he wanted to lean me over a table and fuck the daylights out of me. Then he told me he'd better take me home and we shouldn't do this again (we did).

This is all true, as true as memory, which may reassemble and collage disparate bits into a new (w)hole. I have never told anyone about the times in the car because, though I liked what we did, I was ashamed also, because I didn't think that that was what I was supposed to like. Right from the start sex created an alternative space where men told me things they would never share in another context.

What is trust? I keep coming back to this question because our trust has been damaged. So how can I build a new trust with you? Through stories? Telling you things I've never been able to speak when we are speaking? I loop back around to you. Thinking of you at this distance and imagining you in the ocean and what you smell like afterwards.

Early on, before I knew what this meant, you described how drugs and alcohol in clubs gave you the opportunity to be vulnerable and loving with your male friends. Emotional expression was harder, or impossible even when you were both straight and sober. (I had a moment just now of déjà vu, as if I knew years before we met I wanted to write to you about this ... weird.)

When you and I were in the woods we talked about how getting high was like meeting in a hotel, cheating on reality with each other. You know how attracted I am to alternative realms. I loved meeting you there. Barriers broke down and we told each other what lay beneath. Sometimes it is the sweetest love of all, and sometimes it is hurt.

These metaphoric spaces made real, the shelter made of drugs and alcohol, the shelter of love. And the spaces real in themselves: the interior of a car, a bedroom, a cabin, a tent, a towel over two people's heads at the beach. The various ways we create a little space within our expanse of world. I see you beneath the folds and recognize you and still you are worthy of love. I am too, I tell myself. I told you this before, maybe. About how when I was very sad, I thought if I didn't feel happier by the time I was thirty, I would drown myself in the ocean. It felt like a resolution, but in retrospect it was a vision. I think of our time on the beach. Of you and I. I wasn't waving, but drowning and you came for me. I have never been happier to see anyone than I was seeing you coming over the rocks. I want to keep telling and telling you the truth. What can I do but love you?

A thousand and one kisses,

Celine

60.

Celine had come home from the bus station. Brendan had bought wine. He fucked her in the sweet, rough, and close way he did. They fell asleep and when she woke up he was dressed in his padded denim work coat. He kissed her while she was warm in bed.

In just robe and socks she made coffee and sat down to look at the news. It was his computer that was on the table so she pulled it open. His Gmail came up open. A little edge of doubt made her skim his mail. She wanted to find nothing. But she didn't.

There was someone called Juliette who'd written him four days ago about their weekend together. The email was unbearable, but Celine read it more closely than any text she'd ever consumed. It concluded, "Anyways, just wanted to say I know what you're going through and if you ever want to talk more, I'm here. You know my number, boy."

That was the first crack. Celine felt high, nauseous. She was not in her home anymore—she was in Brendan's kitchen. She had no home. The curtain fluttered because the window was open a crack.

For the rest of the day she scoured his emails and sobbed. She read through everything, searched for her name, for any women's names. All the women they knew. Celine thought cruel things about these women to try to maintain balance, but it was a useless, damaging exercise. She moved into the realm of self-hatred. She felt as if she would die. Wanted to. She thought into a knot, a tangle. There may have been others. More or less. Celine knew these women by sight or by what she had imagined was friendship. Maybe he was pushing her away as a form of cruel test. Maybe if she were another kind of woman he would not have sought out others.

That afternoon he walked in the door as if he knew what she knew, because he did. She looked dead, pale. She asked and he told. In her short absence Brendan had fucked many women, more than Celine could wrap her head around, given the amount of time. Women she knew. Celine in a moment of vertigo realized everyone she knew inhabited Brendan's universe.

In Brendan's kitchen that afternoon the girls rushed out of his mouth and filled the room.

There was Juliette and Rebecca and Kristin. There was also Jessica and Jess, Katie, and Anna.

"But I was only away a little while. It wasn't even a month." She stumbled.

"I thought you were gone for good."

"My clothes were still hanging in the closet. I was writing you everyday. You wrote me. What about all the things you wrote to me, Brendan?"

She asked for details and he gave them like he was very tired. There was Rebecca the fiber artist.

There was Kristin who wore a dog collar and talked about nipple clamps at openings.

Many times Celine had stood next to Brendan at art shows and they'd gossiped in whispers with these women, as if she and Brendan and these women shared some understanding. In those moments Celine had felt arrogantly protected within the relationship.

After those shows she and Brendan would speak skeptically about these women. Rebecca clearly liked to perform her sexuality as an ostentatious form of privilege. People could see that underneath it she was just another boring, rich girl. Kristin was kind of gross. Celine thought they were both trying too hard.

She incanted if if if. She beat her mind with if. If I were another kind of girl he would not have hurt me like this. If I were not the girl with cut marks, too much self-hate, with bit nails and bad jobs. If I loved myself. If I were not a loser. If I were like those cooler girls, like Anna-Rebecca-Kristin-Katie-Juliette-Jess-Jessica with high cheekbones and long, glossy hair, with a career, an art career, a large family, an addiction bravely overcome. If only I were another kind of girl, he would have kept loving me. He wouldn't have treated me like trash.

Now she kept talking as his looks and rages and cigarettes took up their remaining air. Just at the point she felt she would die he would soften and say, "Let's keep talking."

They climbed up the ladder to smoke a joint on the rooftop. He held her under his coat as she sobbed. A western wind blew clouds fast over the city skyline. She ached from crying. Beyond his shoulder there was a line of distant buildings and behind those were more. The black skyscraper and the cluster of silvery ones. Above them planes marked up the sunset clouds with vapor trails. All she wanted was to be alone with him. But it was done. They would never be alone together again.

61.

After the revelation, they tried. He said he wanted to. He said she should stay and they should get married, but then he would go off on some small thing or she would crack and scream curses, sobbing. Her dreams became a tangle of encounters with women. She dreamed exclusively of encounters with Brendan and other women. She would wake up and tell him she loved him without limit.

They stood close in a doorway beside the Skylark after a spring rain had stopped. A train passed above them, its metal-on-metal scream silencing their fight. There was not enough whiskey in the world to calm their troubles. She struggled with the words "I believe." She talked to keep the bubble from bursting. The air needed some magic. Out of desperation she pulled out her most cherished mantra. She could touch his heart and soften the bubble grown brittle.

"I just believe a light protects us. We are protected by it. We only have to trust. I envision you and me surrounded in light together. It is . . ."

He sighed and she stopped. His eyelids were puffy. Truth was told, but not enough or too much. This is karma, she told herself. But drug highs and drunken euphorias and dysphorias made up the true love in which she could be just the other woman.

"I'm not sure I've ever really respected you. You let me fuck you the very first night."

The neon sign above glowed soft red behind layers of winter grime not yet washed away. A group of laughing friends got quiet as they passed. A flight of eyes on them. But then some drunks yelling at one another exited the bar and the spell was broken. Celine had been like these passersby, seeing intimate fights and feeling embarrassed. But things had reversed. It was like the wall of an apartment had been ripped away, making the dolls inside experience the shame of flailing in public. She'd become what she'd once judged.

Another train screamed over their heads. The door of the bar opened and "Wild Horses" bled out. Oh, the yearning in Jagger's voice. Oh, the conviction. This grimy town didn't care for her, but nothing could drag her away, or actually anything could. She pushed her nails into the lifeline on her palm. My love my love my love.

"I love you so much."

"Save some love for yourself."

It was too much. He demanded her love, then threw it back.

"We need to never speak again. You are acting like a child. People break up all the time. We would both be better off. I am so sick of your helpless thinking. You are a grown woman. Act like it. This is not the end of the fucking world. It is wrong. The light you want to see isn't real. All the self-help is fucking useless."

He paused, not on her behalf, but for his own red-faced breath.

"Money is the only thing that's going to protect you. It is what is real. I need some. You need some and that's it. You're a grown woman Celine, act like it. Deal with your issues, get money, and leave me the fuck alone."

62.

Shell shock after heartbreak caused time to scuffle along. Sleep followed waking followed sleep followed waking. Thus time moved. People moved apart.

Celine and Brendan ceased to know one another. There were a few short text messages. She moved out when he was on a trip. Their cat twined around her calves and she wet his fur sticking her teary face into his side. But after that night in front of the Skylark they never again saw one another. Over the summer months Celine sleepwalked through her shitty café job, trying haphazardly to prepare for school, but really all she thought of was the destruction of love. She sang Paul Simon to herself. Everyone can see you're blown apart, she thought.

She lived in a fearful, sick hope that she would see Brendan by chance, but she never did. He seemed to be away, but she knew from friends he wasn't. He'd just turned invisible. He became serious with another woman almost immediately. After learning that, she lived with the fearful anxiety that she would run into him with this new loved woman, but she never did.

63.

A curtain opened and a love walked through. This love was magnetic and created a theatrical space where before only life had been. The stage was a rooftop, or classroom, or gallery. The stage was a café, a kitchen, a bus, a bus stop, a bedroom. Had it been two actors or an endless series of actors playing two characters? Who'd been the audience and who'd been the performer? It remained unclear to her, and this was a flaw.

The sunsets and -rises they'd watched together were gelled lights beamed at a scrim. These bands of quick-shifting reds, bruised purples, and gentle oranges fading incongruously into murky browns and blue-blacks. In her memory two people were together alone. It was only their faith in the performance that kept it passionate, but they did believe and so it was engaged and exciting. This conviction is something we label romantic love. But then we never can be sure how long we'll share the stage with the other. People can't keep one another though they try.

In improvisation the rule is to say "yes."

So when Brendan said, "I want to leave," Celine responded, "Yes, let's go."

But he replied, "You go. I'll go. Separate."

So she stayed and he left. The other, who she'd believed to be her ideal partner and audience, both in one, disappeared. He slammed the flimsy stage door. The flats rocked. The walls were open to the empty seats. She collapsed before no one, but was horribly exposed to herself. She doubted she'd ever been real to him, believing she'd been an object. A prop for a one-man show. She thought, I was not alive to him. I am not alive.

Outside her private pain theater their country continued its various amorphous wars of greed disguised as revenge. Protests rippled through the country, through other countries.

In Mexico, in the city beside her hometown, the cartels and the government warred with one another, both sides using American weapons. So many people died.

Militias and armies warred around the world, both sides using American weapons. Town squares and bedrooms and dance clubs and fields were drenched in blood. Photographers from around the world came to document mothers and sisters and brothers and neighbors collapsing in sobs or else covering their faces.

Sometimes Celine looked at the news on her computer screen, and the settings of the most horrible images were at once foreign and familiar.

It was the end of summer.

64.

Her mother would cry or almost cry on their weekly phone calls as she detailed new indignities, new violences large and small. About how many armed men were at her favorite lunch spot. About how there were new checkpoints on every road out of town. About how a woman she knew who worked at an office downtown had a gun pulled on her.

"One day she took the elevator two floors to the soda machine. She didn't know ICE had moved in."

"What's ICE?"

"Immigration and Customs. The Feds. The guard at the door aimed his gun at her and screamed at her, in the building she's worked in for thirty years!" Celine's mother's voice rose.

"It's so awful," her mother would say over the phone. "Drugs and this fascist war on terror are ripping everything to shreds. But it's nothing compared to what's happening on the other side. The worst corruption. The corrupt government selling out their own people. The multinationals gutting the community so the cartels could just go wild. And then the Mexican president says if you're murdered by the cartel, you were somehow guilty. Such lovely logic! It means no one innocent ever gets murdered. Or rather, if you're murdered, you must have been guilty of something. Does he think everyone implicated in crime deserves the death penalty? Great. Just great. I will tell you. We are a part of this history. No one is innocent, but we still must live. We are all a part of this society. I refuse to accept the fucking logic of all this barbarity just because it's making somebody money.

"And I cannot even tell you about all the murdered women. Now, finally after all these mothers marched and protested *for years*, now they are talking about it. But solving it? No."

As she picked her nails, Celine interjected, "You don't need to yell at me. I'm on your side."

"But sweetheart, it's just so bad. You can't imagine."

"This is what grandma and grandpa feared about Amber but like, actually happening."

"Oh, Celine," her mother hesitated. "You know about Amber's mother, don't you? About Sue?"

"She fucked Amber emotionally. I know that."

"No honey, we might have confused you. We didn't explain."

"So, what?"

"I feel guilty. We neglected such an important point, you were becoming a woman."

"I hate that phrase, 'becoming a woman.'"

"And I was off in another headspace with my own issues."

"I thought Amber died of kidney failure."

"Why did you think that?"

"That's what you told me."

The room got larger sonically as Celine focused on some spider plant shoots quivering in the window. The next-door asshole teenager shouted across the courtyard.

"Well, no. Her kidneys did fail. But not in Mexico, here. We took her to the hospital. That happened a few years before. You should know, given everything that's happened with you.

"But what I don't think you knew, why Amber was so damaged. It wasn't that Sue was a bad mother. Sue was murdered. She was trying, but had struggled so much with drinking and drugs. She was with this man after your uncle. It wasn't him, but he was with a heavier crowd. This is what was behind your grandparents' and my feelings about Amber.

"Amber had such deep addiction problems, and then that boyfriend of hers; he was so good for her. They were in a little beach town the day she died. They fought, and she went to the bar and got drunk. He said she was just crying and crying, saying she wanted her life back. He said they had made up and that they were both drunk and decided to go night swimming. But. The tide had changed, and he was out of it and couldn't rescue her, and she got pulled out against some rocks and . . . drowned."

"Do you think he did that on purpose?"

"No. Absolutely, I don't blame Ollie. He was as damaged as she was. I was like them Celine, when I was young. I was in the same places as Sue. When I was young I was not making the same kind of choices you were making. I was fucking up my life.

"It happened when you were so young and I couldn't bear to talk about it, because of the stuff with your grandparents. I didn't want to burden you with all this tragedy. It was wrong to keep it from you."

"I wasn't that young."

"We all wanted you to have a different path in life. I wanted you to be able to be a different kind of woman. I'm sorry."

65

When Celine hung up the phone her environment rearranged itself until there were no apparent plots, no visible bloodstains. The violence existed for her only in words. In the fridge a box of strawberries sat beside a bag of corn tortillas. She made salad and a quesadilla. A breeze carried in the sound of a baseball game. She changed her outfit and put on moisturizer and perfume. By carefully arranging her appearance, she could—she needed to believe—counteract the ravages of heartbreak. She did not want her ruined insides visible. She biked along side streets to a friend's opening.

For a long time she stood whispering with her friend Caroline in front of a painting of a chair. It was jokey Matisse with IKEA-style potted plants and rose-colored walls. They drank glass after plastic glass of cheap white. Caroline said, "Brendan was an asshole." Celine simultaneously agreed and made excuses. It was her fault. Fuck. She shouldn't cry.

"Listen, this is the lesson: He was vulnerable, so he fucked you over to prove he wasn't."

"Let's not talk about it."

"Fine, let me introduce you to my friend. She's visiting from New York."

The New York friend looked the part, possessing more polish than her Chicago counterparts. It all came down to the details: a blonder bun and higher-heeled clogs, manicured hands at the end of smooth, slim arms. Jessica, that was her name, was a curator. Of course. She seemed genuinely nice. Celine shifted and hunched in her itchy jealousy, as she remembered her teenaged self looking at girls more sophisticated than she knew how to be. She felt like a loser asshole, nevertheless she played nice. She chitchatted. The New Yorker asked where she was from, then got all excited when she answered.

"Oh, the desert is so magical."

Celine had heard this many times from nice people who maintained the desert as a dream space that remained purer than other American realities.

"I spent one summer in Taos doing a residency. Have you been to Ojo Caliente?"

This fantasy was about some Georgia O'Keeffe floral starkness. Healing mud and sun-crackled signs pointing to tiny towns. Cow skulls and yucca flowers. Celine knew the picture. This fantasy was also made real by nice northerners who ran galleries on Santa Fe's Canyon Road. The women who chatted naked in the women-only pool at Ten Thousand Waves. It was real. A beautiful, dusty place where people created a mystic desert for tourists, but also really did do peyote ceremonies and sweat lodges. The real stuff mingled with the postcard image. But what about the strip malls and the diabetes and the nuclear waste? She was, Celine thought of saying, from the shitty border. It's the wrong side of the tracks, metaphorically. You probably didn't go there and if you did, you probably didn't like it. But whatever, she thought. All this thinking took only a few moments while Jessica the New Yorker rhapsodized about all the stars in the navy velvet skies and the Agnes Martin sunrises.

Who was she, Celine wondered, to burst these beautiful art bubbles with her own shitty traumas?

"It does have a special kind of magic," she agreed smiling, while over the speakers came the opening guitar chords of "Gold Dust Woman."

66

Her mother emailed a link, an excerpt from a short novel written by her hometown playwright. His author photo, attached to the literary reviews and interviews, showed he'd grown older handsomely. His hair was silver but still full; he wasn't looking into the camera but beyond. In one interview he talked about a talented student he'd had in the '90s. Her murder, along with the many murders of women across the border had prompted him to write the book. However he was careful never to mention the student's name and to insist that his work was, in the end, one of fiction. Reviewers praised him for his compelling portrait of a young woman in life and death. This was truly a departure for this author who had, in his previous theatrical work, not really taken the female experience into account. In reading it, Celine remembered Donna Beth's little nuances—the ones she knew she and Julie had seen. She had to read through the old man's romantic sketch and her own ideal memory to try to picture the person who had been many years younger when she was murdered than Celine was now. Everyone's fantasy gets piled on top of this dead girl. Who should be speaking up for her?

Celine recognized some of the book as a reworking of his play. Donna Beth was now Laura. In the novel Laura was a balletic Lolita. He made her into a fantasy and didn't have to worry because the real Donna Beth was no longer around to push against the words the playwright was putting into her mouth. At least in the play Celine and Julie had seen the living Donna Beth saying his words in her own cracked voice.

For a performance class Celine decided to present the writer's version of Donna Beth's death monologue. Celine decided she would lip-sync to a recording she made. In art speak she was reappropriating his appropriation and thus, by collapsing the controlling traditionally masculine figure of the writer director and the traditionally more passive feminine figure of the actress muse, she was subverting his bid for control. In her private speak Celine was exposing his gross morbid bid to control the story of a girl the old man had once secretly fucked. She wasn't sure she was less guilty than him, but at least she was injecting shame into his text. It was as lacking as it was needed.

To prepare, Celine wrote a series of questions for herself. Who do dead bodies belong to? Who do women's bodies belong to? Are women beings or objects? Is there something between?

On the day of the performance she straightened her hair and dressed in some approximation of the 1990s style: a rose cotton tank, sailor jeans, an evil eye choker, eyes ringed with black kohl.

She stood in the middle of the curtained stage. Her friend turned on the single spotlight, as Celine had instructed. She took a beat and a deep breath. She began to move as the recording of playwright-as-Donna Beth began:

"Over the course of my life, photos of me appeared three times in the *Sun-News*. Each was an encounter with a wider audience." Behind her a slideshow of doubling figures began. There were Rivette women, Lynch women, and Altman women. There were shadows, reflections, and decisive moments.

"The first was when I got on the honor roll senior year. There were rows of tiny headshots of all the good students. Little face splotches in black and white."

Celine could make out her twenty classmates in the auditorium by the reflective circles of people's glasses and their dark silhouettes.

"The second photo was much bigger. It was me as Peter Pan in flight. I remember that shoot. Smiling 'naturally' for a long time while the photographer fussed."

Her teacher, a bird of a woman with big glasses, nodded and moved her gaze back and forth between Celine and her legal pad, making notes for critique.

Her recorded voice continued, "The last photo was a glamor shot of me in my prom dress. My mom made me pose to please my grandparents. My grandmother has that framed photo on her living room wall next to a photo of my mom when she was younger."

Through this performance Celine was trying to say . . . what? She interrogated and answered herself. Explain yourself. Women's bodies belong to themselves, but that is denied so forcefully we deny it to ourselves. I am a material being and in between. Dead bodies belong to the world according to who? This is an affirmation of love and a push to make meaning out of our nervous system.

"Now there's a shrine below both our images. It is a little table draped in a blue velvet scarf, with candles in cut-glass angel-shaped holders, crystals, silk flowers, and prayer cards. My grandma's taste was always tacky."

Celine was crying, angry with herself for doing so. In rehearsals she'd been able to get through the whole piece calmly. Now before an audience, she felt like she was violating Donna Beth's privacy. Who was she to be doing this? Fuck. But there was no way out but through. The recorded voice continued.

"I was stoned that afternoon. My boyfriend and I had gotten high and had sex after my cashiering shift at Toucan's. James and I were saving to move to LA at the end of that summer. It was supposed to be our last summer in the land of entrapment. I remember being super-happy and super-impatient.

"I should have known. I should have, with that just-washed black Dodge Ram Charger behind my mom's Tercel.

"I did know, actually, only I didn't drive away. I parked, but didn't get out. I could have. I strained to hear voices inside, but there were none. It had already occurred and was about to happen. I depressed the lighter. Counted backwards for the time of a cigarette. Supernatural hearing. My teacher said acting is listening."

Celine felt this performance was the torture she deserved, never really having been a good actress like Julie or Donna Beth. It wasn't that she lacked conviction; it's just she didn't have that good actor ability to be both open and present while staying in control of her emotions. Her instincts didn't serve the pressure of the stage. She was simultaneously too uncomfortable in the present and already elsewhere. The recorded voice kept on.

"My mother liked her plot of land because there was a lot of space between her and the neighbors. A kiddy pool for their grandkids beneath a cottonwood tree, some chaparral, and a pile of bricks for a patio my stepfather had been threatening to lay for years, but never did.

"My mom's neighbor recognized the Ram too. When mother and son heard, they were sitting in the swamp-cooler air, half-watching *Terminator* with the boys to pass time. That night the sheriff stood in the kitchen, asking her questions; she noticed the casserole of enchiladas was half-eaten. She cried as they talked.

"'I could hear them fighting about something from all the way over here. I could hear her screaming curses sometimes and I thought, this is no good. When he moved out she was hysterical. But then it got quiet and I thought it was better. Ester was a nice lady and her daughter didn't do anything to deserve this. It is so awful. Just so awful. They are with God now.' And the neighbor's son and the sheriff tried to comfort her, but she could not be comforted because she had seen that trailer so like her own, soaked in blood so like her own. The things you don't see coming. As the neighbor wept she said, 'I must have known already from when I first saw him. He was a bad man.' The sheriff said, 'It is not the sort of thing people were good at predicting.'

"When the neighbor opened the door she saw my body first.

"My stepfather punched me when I walked in. My mother's body was in her bedroom, naked below the waist. My stepfather had raped my mother before he shot her. I could tell. He did the same to me. He choked me while he was doing it. Then held his gun to my head and fired. I died in my blood."

Celine looked at her audience, lasering energy towards them.

"Only after killing the women he'd called 'lover' and 'like a daughter' did he turn the gun on himself."

This happens everywhere. Women double-killed, visible and invisible.

"This is a shard of the real," she mouthed, diverging from the script.

Finally it ended. In her mind she pictured Brendan and Julie, her intended absent audience.

Celine could no longer see, but she felt when the lights went out.

67

At school a pale, thin man with a buzz cut sat in the semi-darkness with other professors, looking at Celine as she attempted to articulate something about the colonial violence perpetrated by her culture and country. She struggled to trace the line between comfort and complicity. "We feel we are a good people from a good country," Celine said. "Even when the evidence suggests otherwise. The greatest trick of any system is to become invisible to those inside."

She was trying to sift through poisonous garbage imagery without becoming another producer or unintentional celebrant of the toxins. How does one handle this stuff? How does one turn poison into medicine?

"But we're all inside this mess, aren't we?"

She pushed forward with the slideshow that was projected on the screen behind her. In the dark the professor looked at her sour.

She said she was trying to figure out if she was a witness or a participant. Was she a participant/observer or a scavenger feeding on the carnage that Google Image Search provided? Poisoning her mind with violence in order to call for reforms. She, like so many, found herself calling for the destruction of patriarchal, racist, global capitalism. She found herself making this cry for reform haphazardly and without the proper tools. Just another girl making performance art for a psychic revolution.

The man in the semi-darkness twitched, dissatisfied with the mess he was witnessing. He taught animation. His own work involved painstakingly shooting still images and objects to give them the illusion of motion. In Europe his work was praised for its control.

In the Midwest he was tasked with overseeing undergraduate and graduate students as they made their own animated work. He sat on committees. He critiqued. He was the outside eye there to witness and give impartial feedback to young artists like Celine. It would be a cheap shot to say he looked miserable—lips pinched, and dressed in a uniform of baggy neutrals—but he did.

He sighed heavily.

He said, "First off, the idea that this is all our fault is some kind of liberal fantasy."

He was her enemy. This is what she had to fight against.

68.

One afternoon, after it had been raining, Celine walked along the river crying from heartbreak. The night before she had taken mushrooms. The residual sensations were still present. Clouds and sunlight piled over the lake, puffy, slanted, sublime. The whole city was a boat.

To escape from herself she ducked into a movie theater. Drug hangover plus her heart-raw feeling made her empathetic towards everything: the gold, red, and black velvety art deco lobby, the theater, and the other audience members.

She felt peaceful and present and yet voluptuously sad. Brendan was beside her, she imagined. Everything is so useless and beautiful. People are just themselves and our expectations are fantasies that have nothing to do with them, she thought. So simple and so complicated.

The film was about a German man. When he was a very small child at the end of WWII, he saw fighter planes destroying his city, but he was not afraid. He wanted to be a pilot so when he grew up he moved to the US and joined the military. It was the 1960s by then, so they sent this young pilot to Vietnam, where he was shot down, then captured. The Cambodian soldiers tied a wasp nest to his head to torture him.

She sat in the old red velvet theater—high, sort of high—and wept because the jungle trees in the film of the place she had never been were beautiful. The film was so full of leaves and wind and light and survival and the most subtle acts of resistance and generosity and cruelty all at once. As she watched she wondered: how can I love and want love this bad and be so separate and alone?

In the film the man survives, but is changed, damaged. He returns, but to what? He is an enemy a friend an enemy a friend.

Celine walked back to the empty apartment that wasn't hers and sobbed herself unconscious.

69.

After making coffee but before committing to the day, she curled up fetal in her borrowed bed.

This bedroom faced Western Avenue. She had no idea if it was accurate, but she liked to imagine that this broad road, full of semis barreling through lights, ran all the way to the southern and northern borders. Maybe this road was a straight line sewing together Mexico, the US, and Canada. She thought of the concentrate of the country she carried inside like it was a swallowed drug. She was a mule carrying American poison. She was an English-speaking wanderer with a burst balloon inside, with deadly contents seeping. She could not feel patriotic, but could offer love and recognition to a violated place. She did not belong to the desert, but had nowhere else to go. Celine choked on tears.

In New Mexico, hot-air ballooning was popular. She recalled her father explaining how the appeal had to do with the landscape's vast, treeless expanses and the rapid shifts of temperature. Cold nights gave way to hot mornings, something to do with air pressure. Ballooning was a thing, a pastime for people with extra money—the equivalent of owning a boat in a place with water. There was a fiesta every year up in Albuquerque.

At ten or eleven she'd been up in a balloon with her father. They'd gotten up in the freezing dark in order to get to the launch in time. Her father had brought a thermos of hot chocolate, but she'd still grumbled.

The balloon had risen with a flaming whoosh. That and the fear of falling had been so intense she'd clamped her eyes closed and her arms around her fathers arm until they were far up.

"Look" he'd coaxed. "It's beautiful Celine." She'd relaxed long enough to peek. The desert had been made a smooth blanket. Death felt so possible. The father and daughter drifted in a red and yellow balloon as the sun came over the mountains. There was the faintest breeze; they drifted south. The burner created heat shimmers above their heads.

Why am I still alive, she wondered, pressing her tear-wet cheek into the pillow. Her lids had swelled so much it was hard to see, but out the window was the same cold, clear sky. It was a different cold, clear day.

4.

Tromp L'Oréal

The Young-Girl　　　　　　*Identical in this*
is an instrument　　　　　　*to the alienated social*
in service to a general politics　*whole*
of the extermination　　　　*the Young-Girl*
of beings　　　　　　　　*hates sorrow*
capable　　　　　　　　*because sorrow*
of love　　　　　　　　　*condemns her*
　　　　　　　　　　　　just as it condemns
　　　　　　　　　　　　this society.

—Tiqqun

1.

In the girls' hometown the smell of roasting chilis fills the fall air. In winter, only light coats are needed. Winds whip springs and burning rays blanch summers. Old buildings are made of dried mud bricks and newer buildings of stacked cinderblock or framed walls stuccoed. In the nicer neighborhoods, homeowners pay landscapers to fill their yards with volcanic rock and cacti, because water is too precious for lawns. In poorer neighborhoods, people beat the dust hard by parking cars out front. Kids cough. Elbows crack and the backs of necks go brown beneath the sun.

In the girls' hometown the pecan orchards grow in grids. In spring farmers flood them and the water reflects the sky, making an optical illusion, a world mirror.

Next to one orchard there is a rowboat stuck in the sand. Who knows how it got there. The girls like to sit in this boat. It is one of their secret spots.

2.

Every few miles along the border is an officer in an SUV. During the day they sit drinking truck stop coffee out of Styrofoam. After lunch silvery paper wrappings of burgers or burritos lay balled on the dash. At night they spike a fresh coffee with an airline-sized bottle of alcohol. Whatever it takes to keep alert. Each officer is in radio contact with partners. Their headlights penetrate the desert.

3.

By magic or design, disaster is expected. To expect is to call into being.

4.

A fata morgana playing across the highway creates a vertical stack of images.

There appears to be a red velvet curtain. A spotlight is switched on and two girls step into its circle. One is dressed in a pair of cutoffs and a T-shirt that reads "Here comes trouble." The other has on a man's jacket over her mini-dress. Their faces are puffy like they'd just been crying, or drinking. Maybe both.

Both.

They address their audience. By speaking, they begin to make themselves human. These are girls not as bodies, not as parts, but as humans being alive. It is amazing this must be said, but it must. Such recognition is not a given; it is a fight.

5.

"Call us Celine and Julie.

"Those are not our real names, but ones we like. Names worthy of girls worthy of desire. We assumed them from characters in our favorite film. Think of us as the understudies.

"Celine and Julie are sinners fleeing ennui. What grips their insides is knowledge of their value, their worthlessness. They flee because, in their world, existence hinges on a litany of imperatives. Be pretty, charm, adapt to threat. The lessons might be summarized as *Be good or else.*

"In rejecting this, Celine and Julie go towards the unknown, gripped by fever, tormented by remorse, but forever pure in their vices, forever human as we are. The harms Celine and Julie perpetrate are mostly against themselves, but they believe these actions have a higher purpose.

"In risking themselves, they try to save others. Selves future past. They live their lives caught in messes of afternoon obsessions and delights. They wear their vices airbrushed on

T-shirts—*Laugh now, cry layers. The world is (y)ours.*

"If we had been born men you would call on genius ghosts to validate our sins.

"But Celine is not Céline and Julie is not Baudelaire. Girls are not Genets, you degenerate. Cruces is no Paris, and there is no way we are gonna make it to the end of this night."

Celine and Julie roll their eyes across the Dodge Ram Charger's deep-blue interior. They repeat the spell that starts the play afresh.

"You have to rite or remain silent."

The moonlike spotlight fades to black.

6.

Lights up.

Chaos and panic bounces around what appears to be a calm ranch-style home. But the domestic sphere is always furnished with emotional strife, reified.

In the bedroom, a plastic bottle of aloe gel, a pair of striped cotton socks with one tucked over the other to make a single ball, a Fossil watch, a few small bobby pins threaded onto another larger bobby pin, Kiss My Face Peaches & Crème lotion, rose otto oil, the Samuel French edition of *Top Girls*, a *Sassy Magazine* August issue, a *Seventeen Magazine* September issue, cassettes of Nevermind, Under the Pink, and Nothing's Shocking.

After making a cup of coffee and putting jam on bread, the mom turns to the TV where oil wells burn and crowds chant. After a commercial for pain medication the news flickers with an account of a girl who went out but never came home.

At some moment the home stage becomes too small to hold girl passions.

7.

I wanted something bigger   That's what she said
Shut up idiot

8.

Julie got into theater because she had an ineffable spark and high cheekbones, Celine because she needed to pretend to survive.

9.

A pair of headlights bob over the bad ground of a hill on the edge of town. The vehicle moves along the dirt road for some time before the driver decides he's found a stopping place hidden from the highway. One would have needed to be going to the empty livestock water tank at midnight to find them.

So no one knows where she is except this man. She's gone with him knowing she cannot trust him. He has swagger and is fun at parties, but is also manic and guilt-ridden because his Christian upbringing tangles with his desire to fuck pretty girls and get all twisted. She's heard him praying for forgiveness in the bathroom before doing lines with friends in the living room.

Inside the parked truck next to the livestock water tank is a girl and an erratc man.

She knows better, but there she is.

A hand on her back　　　　An image feeling
Get into it　　　　　　　This is method acting
Repetition of an image feeling　The blue plush seat
prickles her cheek.

The girl with a hand on her neck gags, but this only makes him push harder. She knows she has to pretend so it can become real. He moves her body. Through the windshield she sees how the dark behaves like a curtain.

Far off there are fireworks, but she knows they aren't made from gunpowder.

She reverses her mind so she can see the holes. Foreground and background shift. Behind the night's curtain is another screen of sequined gold.

As he chokes her she thinks, everything is more beautiful when you know it will come to an end.

10.

A girl　　　　　　　　Who got sort of raped
just had to shrug it off　　Whatever

11.

Onstage actors flicker between object and being. During the rehearsal period they are touched, measured and assessed, blocked and directed.

Actors scrutinize text and timing as they do their best to realize their director's vision.

When the play is on they move their costumed bodies

through light and shadow. The best actors give in and become reflective surfaces below which their own humanity moves.

Theater is their truest school. Its central lesson is that every performance exists within another, greater one.

12.

The body of the girl is discovered on the floor covered with a blanket, in a house made of wood and cardboard. The body is discovered on top of a truck tire in an empty lot. The body is inside a vehicle of a recent year. She is facedown with legs bent, without panties, pants, or shoes.

The body showed visible signs of having been murdered. She has a bloody nose and bits of glue from adhesive tape stuck to her skin.

She had been a barmaid at the nightclub Day and Night. She had been an employee at the General Hospital's laundry service. She had been on her way to a meeting for vendors of beauty products.

She had been named Juliette.

13.

The police arrive
Beepers blow up
Phones ring and ring

14

Celine and Julie, dressed in makeshift mourning, wait on the church's brown grass. Neither own much black so they've had to borrow clothes from their mothers. No one is prepared for this death.

Friends and aunts and uncles and cousins emerge from the service. She was young and murdered. Doubly tragic. The mourners cry and cling together.

At the wake people get drunk to cope.

Those who find alcohol insufficient supplement. They get high beneath the dark-green pines out back and do bumps off keys in the bathroom. Solutions of sorts.

The grief doesn't leave, but the mourners temporarily pool their sadness. The shared grief sloshes around the house and flows through lungs, hearts, and rib cages.

15.

Law & Order was the longest running crime drama on American primetime television. The girls are ten when it begins and thirty when it ends. The show weaves through childhood and adulthood like a spun thread.

16.

The show presents crimes as singular instances that are tragic but solvable. The focus is on investigation and prosecution. The show says that police and DAs represent the people as an abstract entity. Specific people also appear as victims, witnesses, and perpetrators, but these are all just guest stars circling around the steady twin poles of police and lawyers.

On this show, at least, police have the will to find the true perpetrators, and lawyers have the will to bring true justice.

What kind of monster would do this? they ask as they take over from victims; the crime is their story now.

Almost always the perpetrator is introduced in the first ten minutes, but neither victims nor perpetrators elicit deep feeling. They are ciphers. Burglary, beating, rape, murder ripped from the headlines: whatever had happened is flattened by rhythmic telling about cops and lawyers. A comforting story structure about a state functioning against the chaos of violence.

17.

The girls prefer *X-Files*. They like the romantic tension between Scully and Mulder, the occult plotlines, and the moody Northwest scenery. They like the fantasy of uncovering cover-ups. But it is *Law & Order*'s thump that gently hammers its way into the girls' consciousness. Years later, the opening music cues a wash of involuntary memories.

18.

In the costume shop the girls are taught how to identify fabric by how it frays or burns. The flame from muslin is not the same color as from rayon. Broadcloth produces a different ash than silk. The petroleum-based fabrics don't so much burn as melt into drops which, when cool, resemble beads of crude oil.

19

Whether inside or away from the theater, the girls act out.

They play repetitive games of hair and body, skin and clothes. They perform rituals like getting high before wandering through the mall's bubble of air conditioning, Clinique, and Obsession. They decide to go to a movie at the Cineplex.

The girls have a favorite thrift store they frequent for its soft '80s cardigans and worn-down cowboy shirts. The lady who runs it has a 50%-off sale the second Friday of each month. She is an old Texan, with a white perm and a dog that looks like her hair except for the two, shiny eyes peeping out of the its tear-stained pouf of a head.

One sale day the girls, laughing, are trying on beaded prom dresses, tulle prom dresses, and some relic bridal gown, when they hear the old Texan say, "Feminazis cause trouble. If they're so worried they should learn how to act around men, not the other way round."

After that the girls shift their allegiances to the by-the-pound animal rescue charity shop.

Julie draws wings on her eyelids. Celine hennas her hair red like Angela Chase. Beneath panties pubic hair pushes through their skin as if their skin was a fine mesh.

Meteorologically speaking, *verga* is an observable streak or shaft of precipitation that falls from a cloud but evaporates or sublimes before it reaches the ground. It is commonly seen in the desert and other temperate climates.

In Spanish the equivalent for cock is *verga*. The equivalent for penis is *pene*. Verga is much more rude. Verga can also be used kind of like telling someone to go fuck off. It is like a nonexistent place where you send someone.

22.

Their teen years correspond with the passage of NAFTA. This doesn't mean much to them until later, but across the border, the city grows. Factories bring young people to the city. Bosses express a preference for young women because they are dexterous and better behaved than men. The factories promise a better future to their workers and deliver cheap goods to their consumers.

In that era the city across the border is called City of the Future as a compliment.[1]

23.

The old period blurs into the next one just beginning. The era doesn't have its name yet. The selvage edges of empires begins to fray even as they are being stitched together. Fresh blood comes out.

In those years the murders are treated as discrete occurrences.

24.

In secret the girls cut their arms and hips into strips the way they've been taught to cut fabric.

What fabric are they made of? Not muslin, not velvet either. Maybe some kind of cotton.

Something sheer and soft, but not that soft.

25.

Celine and Julie start at the local college. They can study because they don't have to work at factories. By birth they are lucky, because they were born on the rich side of the border and born into a class where college is the sanctioned entry point into successful adulthood. They walk across the quad to the new library, which is cool and smells like off-gassing industrial carpet.

26.

In college they take art and history and literature and political science classes. They read about how rapid urbanization and industrialization fomented revolutions.

They listen to teachers describe the dream and catastrophes of modernity.

"Taylorization," say their teachers.

"Dada," they say, and also, "psychoanalysis."

"The Cold War and the military industrial complex."

"Semiotics."

The girls mark key words in pink and blue highlighter on the page.

"This is a summary," say their teachers. "I am making sweeping generalizations about what you are reading. Understand it is much more nuanced than I can get into here."

27.

The girls stop acting for philosophical reasons.

They think they can escape the molds and types of femininity presented and represented in theater. No more ingénues or shrews, wenches or grandes dames. Better to be than to act, because one takes the shape of what one performs.

They are lifting the veil, they think as they duck under soft folds.

28.

Despite the heady concepts and study groups, college also has a normal amount of casual sex and sexual coercion, drug use, drunk driving, and boredom.

A boy asks if she wants to study at his place and they end up hooking up. While he tries to make her come, a truck alarm begins its distracting bleat in the parking lot outside. She drifts while trying not to hear herself think.

Car alarms are the love songs of their generation.

29.

The girls' eyes swim in dust and heat reflections that rise off the highway—a mesmerizing instability.

30.

The police agree amongst themselves these girls were prostitutes, or engaged in the drug trade, or Lolitas flirting with trouble, dangerously half-alive.

Publically, the police call for calm, faith in the system.

"We are looking into the chasm of each murder. We will find the responsible party. We ask for your cooperation. Rain will break the drought. The clouds will clear when the wind picks up."

31.

The girls thought the feeling of suffocation was particular to their town.

They learn later it was not.

Using the language of logic and values of the West, the girls criticize their home. It is a coping mechanism.

The mall is a grotesque hall of boredom, and strip malls are just sad. They parrot their teachers' criticism of local government plans to give developers free rein. What about making something actually livable here? This city sucks, they add. This desert is treated as nothing but a garbage dump for nuclear waste. Why couldn't they have been born in Europe, the girls lament. They learn to hate their West as they fall for another. Western Civilization, true West.

This is a shitty place, they agree, preparing to leave.

So tired, so eager, and just eighteen years old.

There is no peace in whatever.

32.

Seen from the air, what disappears from the desert are the fine traces of life, small but pungent leaves, jackrabbits, yucca flowers.

168

The last visual elements to disappear from view are broad strokes of geology and human industry laid bare: asphalt lines across dust, kidney-shaped turquoise swimming pools surrounded by dust, military fences, car lot fences, backyard fences, factory fences, and the border—the hardest fence of all, dividing dust from more dust.

33.

Julie finds herself a new, altogether different West, the one that hugs the deep, dark, shining Pacific. The city is an international theme park of naturalness, with beaches and condos and in the distance, shipping vessels.

She wanders through a mix of old and new influences, North American, European, and Asian investment properties. She sees actual killer whales leaping out of the literal sea, just like on a tourism brochure.

It is the best place on earth, people say. They shot the *X-Files* and *Scooby* 2 here. It's called Hollywood North.

She waits for her friend Ayden in front of Science World's geodesic dome as casino lights shimmer on the surface of False Creek.

Women run past her along the seawall, hurrying their yoga bodies away from anxiety. She feels jealous of their useless, loping beauty.

34.

Celine makes her way first into the alien world full of wide trees that rustled and bear fruit. She lives through seasons she'd seen before only on TV. She attends rock shows and film festivals and bikes through traffic jams.

This world is so full of fashionable shops with expensive desirable dresses, and sandals, and hoodies, and gold hoops. It is full of restaurants with patios where they serve sangria. It is full of old men who play bocce in the park and who watch soccer games at coffee shops. It is full of walk-up apartments and fire escapes and rooftop parties and people who travel and study and work not just dead-end jobs, but career jobs, like radio producer or architect. For a long time cities are nothing but spectacular to Celine.

35.

They realize they never learned what they were supposed to do once they grew up. Perhaps they had skipped that lesson to smoke weed and giggle with boys.

36.

The girls rush into more learning, more experience. The panic beneath the surface comes from fear of death before living a real life. Call it depression or anxiety.

Study and work and shows and parties and art and movies. They attend lectures and roundtables and debates. They learn so much; to think about themselves as if from the outside.

37.

Over semesters they study interiors and exteriors, waves of feminism, colonialism and post-colonialism, resistance and redefinitions, masculinity and femininity and the force of binaries, queer politics and poetry, minimalism and post-minimalism, affect and trauma, and labor and leisure. The girls take notes and examine their speech and actions.

38.

Polite, well-educated capitalists desecrate sublime land-scapes around the world. Slaughterhouses, weapons plants, and cloth factories pumping dye waste into rivers means jobs, say the capitalists.

Their teachers tell the girls about how a sick spiral of overpro-duction and overconsumption decreases the value of human workers. They theorize about how this is also happening with images, and objects remaking images, and objects producing desire for more images and objects, while decreasing the plea-sure people feel with their images and objects.

It sounds like a riddle because it is one.

39.

They read that women are the archetypal consumer and product of modernity. They are the shopper and the shop girl, the factory girl and the whore. They are at the core of this big project as makers, consumers, and products.

40.

They read the Individual—in the European conception of the Individual—is dying.

They read their country—their generation—is also dying.

Sick, but still walking. They read they have been raised on poisonous garbage.

They read how it is the fault of the weak yet powerful Other. It is the fault of the media, or it is perhaps due to the feminization of the culture, that the strong autonomous Individual is dying.

But, the critics hasten to add, when we say feminization we are not referring to actual women.

41.

The girls fall in love with different men, but at many turns they find themselves estranged. Estrangement seems to be an epidemic, but it is couched either as an ability to compartmentalize or a fear of intimacy caused by divorced parents. The girls are encouraged to love, but warned they will not get much in return. The girls never feel like individuals even when they feel totally alone. They want to share with the men soft states of loving togetherness and suffer when men can't or won't go with them.

The emotions the men cannot feel lead them to states of apathy, depression, and rage. They feel those emotions freely.

Sometimes the girls feel confused or quietly devastated. Sometimes they scream back, and sometimes they watch the men punch holes in walls or throw patio furniture into their complex's swimming pool.

42.

Julie meets a friend for a walk. They struggle to find a path around the construction sites as her friend describes a film about neoliberal violence.

43.

Men in theory classes say through implication that the girls don't quite grasp the difficult concepts.

But, they continue, the girls have some interesting questions and perhaps will one day understand, if they continue studying.

44.

The girls read, "Male identity . . . emphasizes only one side of the balance of differentiation—difference over sharing, separation over connection, boundaries over communion, self-sufficiency over dependence."[2]

45.

The forceful splitting of emotion and intellect, reason, and feeling.

Maybe this is what the system working sounds like.

46.

While haunting the library they come across alternative texts that bolster their own hidden feelings.

They read, "At the height of being in love the boundary between ego and object threatens to melt away. Against all the evidence of his senses, a man who is in love declares that 'I' and 'you' are one, and is prepared to behave as if it were a fact."[3]

The girls yearn for unmediated, alive connections.

47.

Books tell the girls that they love others hopelessly not because it is natural, but because centuries of culture hinged on their devotion to individual men and the systems of men. Girls are made to exist only in relation to others. The culture teaches them to find their life purpose in caring for others.

48.

The girls try to be reasonable even as they wonder how mind and body can be separate. We have bodies but also are bodies. Right?

They remember their mothers' copies of *Our Bodies, Ourselves*.

Mothers, the book they are reading says, are not seen by their boy children, "as an independent person (another subject) but as something other—as nature, as instrument or object, as less than human. The premise of this independence is to say, 'I am nothing like the one who cares for me.' In breaking this identification with . . . mother the boy is in danger of losing his capacity for mutual recognition all together."[4]

49.

This is a play about men rejecting their mothers and subsequent women in order to differentiate themselves from the oceanic sensations of primal love as first represented by the mother. Love sensations are felt to be an existential threat to singular identity.

50.

If women and girls are seen as objects that arouse deep troubling feelings, then society can justify using them for pleasure and comfort then destroying them. Just look at how we treat the object world.

Threats to singular identity are more often than not met with violence.

51.

Celine sits on the shag carpet hugging a man while he sobs.

He chokes out, "I can't feel anything."

He cries that he loves her but he feels so fucking fucked.

Tears spot her green T-shirt. He seems so alone, as if she is not there.

Celine feels there is nothing but feeling, and she holds him as a way of saying they are not single entities but beings enmeshed in space and touch and pheromones and empathetic connection.

She says their private joke to soften him, "I love you so, monster boyfriend."

52.

A man Julie loved says, "One of my problems is that women fall in love with me too easy," and she sees this is true when he turns his attention away from her and towards another. He has no trouble finding women to care for him.

53.

That summer they see a swan fight a raccoon for bread in the park. In the fall smoke from a forest fire, many miles away, clouds an otherwise clear sky. Over the winter heavy rain overfills the reservoir, rendering tap water temporarily brown and undrinkable. They go dancing a lot that spring.

54.

While in Canada Julie hears Americans on the news saying they will move north should the president get reelected. She rolls her eyes. As if it were so easy to escape your national karma. As if the Canadians want you.

The president gets reelected.

55.

In the glassy West Coast metropolis where VANOC is hard at work preparing for the games, a mass murder case breaks into public consciousness. People described the site of the murders as Canada's ground zero. Bodily materials mingled with the site of violence. It was bad, that bad.

Shockingly so.

56.

The murderer has a name like a weapon. He had been killing women for at least a decade undetected. His face is as terrifying as one might imagine it to be. He is Bob-like, Lynchian.

57

The news coverage trafficks in a kaleidoscope of narratives.

Reporters activate whichever figure or signifier suits the moment. This man is a monster because he had a toxic childhood. Or he experienced humiliation at the hands of a prostitute and was exacting revenge. Or he is a dangerous sociopath unable to experience empathy. Or some people are just evil.

Experts analyze his speech and stringy, ash-colored hair.

58

The girl mind has girl trauma and a girl theory on the subject at hand. The girl has been thinking over classic characters and tropes and structures. It has to be some simple horror story. Simple as dense horror.

What are the chances that the girls would live so close to two sites of the slow-motion mass murder of girls?

What are the chances?   Good I guess

The police had been hearing for years about disappearing women.

Though they should have been looking into these cases, the cops were blinded by their own bias against First Nations, against the poor, against the addicted.

Years before, the man had been arrested and questioned about an attack. A woman said he stabbed her. She fought back and escaped. But because of her drug use and sex work, the police didn't believe her. The police released the farmer.

Why hadn't they taken her seriously? Well, it was complicated.

Complicated because the girls were itinerant wanderers in bad parts of town.

60.

As reporters write it, the girls are simultaneously blameless victims and fools asking for trouble. In life these girls exist within constellations of johns, pimps, wife beaters, boyfriends, sugar daddies, rapists, bad parents, state and community services. It is not unusual for girls like them to disappear. The case is super-horrific, thus a sensation. It has details worse than one can imagine or details exactly like one has come to expect.

61.

Stabbed   Stop
And her stained clothing
And a .22 caliber revolver with an attached dildo
                                          Please stop. Please
But it's in my head

62.

Mourners murmur into one another's necks as they hold one another so as not to drown in feeling.
Murmur names, murmur memories murdered
This cannot go on as this goes on.
This cannot go on as this goes on and on.

Girls who knew the dead girl say,
"We don't want to live anymore. We don't want to live."
The victim's name repeated makes a dirge.

63.

Anxiety and grief stalk through the courtroom.

The judge says, "I think this trial may expose jurors to evidence that will be as bad as a horror movie, and you won't have the option of shutting off the TV."[5]

64.

Precious, expensive, worked over, raw and refined education. Never enough but too much. The girls study as if it is their job, as if it matters. The girls work for money as an afterthought and thus they become overeducated poor.

65.

In this world   there are two kinds
of girls   Celine and Julie are neither

66.

One summer Julie puts on a snorkel mask to see long-legged, ink-colored crabs walking over neon starfish in cold inlet water.

Time zones away Celine picks currants from a bush. The organic farmers had hung CDs so the rainbow light reflections would scare away birds.

She watches a hand-sized lizard bask on a stone step, her sense of the animal merging with a radio voice as it says, Whenever economic trends fail to flow with theory, observers invoke liquidity, in the same way that physicists invoke dark matter to explain problems with the origins of the universe.

67.

At age eleven Celine wore a black armband to be like her mother and her mother's friends who were protesting the Gulf War. On their TVs oil wells burned and a slick black horse wandered out of the desert towards the camera and to a death beyond the frame. In town, plastic yellow ribbons trembled on the trees around the Holiday Inn parking lot.

68.

Celine is visiting her parents during a break from graduate school the first time she hears of Abu Ghraib prison.

She is in her parent's truck in the parking lot of Sutherland's Hardware store, listening to the radio while waiting for her dad to buy whatever home improvement thing he needs.

The announcer describes the sexual nature of the violence enacted on prisoners. He says guards would play heavy metal and country music to keep the prisoners awake for days on end. He describes photos of naked shackled men menaced by dogs. American soldiers point and laugh with open mouths.

69.

Going to keep on	asking
until we get	what we want
What	do you want?
We want	the truth

70.

The girls are still young and therefore still shocked, as if this hadn't happened before, as if it was going to stop.

71.

Julie sits in the library and writes a thesis about out-of-date TV as the fall blurs into winter and the winter into spring. More than TV, the thesis is about young people enmeshed in the mystery of trauma.

Or something.

When asked at parties, she explains away the work with embarrassment. She and her friends joke about their varying levels of unemployability.

72.

She writes about the red curtains in the Black Lodge. She describes how characters get there by passing through a grove of trees marked with a pool of motor oil.

The Black Lodge is "the shadow-self of the White Lodge. The legend says that every spirit must pass through there on the way to perfection. There, you will meet your own shadow-self."[6]

73.

In the fictional worlds of her obsession, characters twin. The murdered-girl cipher Laura had surviving friends who resembled one another. Audrey and Donna and Madeline all have dark curls. Laura and Shelley and Annie are blonds.

Wandering our fantasies are so many amnesiac girls trying to reassemble events from nights before. There are so many broken boys, bereft mothers, mad fathers, and troubled lawmen.

74.

Girl survivors are main characters in this drama. They are friends and rivals, reckless with undigested grief. They too have walked by the same traps, flirted with the same boys, ridden in the same cars. They wonder what kept them alive. What made the murdered girl different?

75.

Notes accumulate in Moleskines, building towards something cohesive.

Trauma leads to "irrational thinking or thought distortions. They may take the form of recurrent images, obsessive ideas, hallucinations, nightmares or short-circuiting of the abstract thinking process."[7]

76.

Trauma leads to "the severing of heart connections, losing the trust necessary to love or to accept being loved. The sexually traumatized child often learns that she is to put everyone's needs before her own. In time, she learns that she has no legitimate needs."[8]

77.

Our world is full of allegories about trauma.

The runaway boy never wants to grow up.

An alien presence who may invade the home makes night terrifying.

The prom queen knows an evil spirit possesses her father.

The bad man is so difficult to see, but just a glimpse makes the children scream and scream.

The abused see the secret hinted at everywhere.

78.

Please believe me.

79.

The girls are told it is a fun thrill to consume images of estranged, dismembered bodies similar to their own. The exquisite corpse makes a good art game.

The horror genre.

80

In the traditional procedural, the police seek knowledge and stability, but in alternate noir forms, the detective is confused and unbalanced.

Noir stories place vulnerable anti-heroes at their centers.

These investigators are often set against the shadow parts of government that they are sworn to represent.

Alternative detectives practice yoga and enter trance states.

They want to believe.

81.

In asking questions, the danger is that investigators may end up investigating—entering—their own roles as potential criminals.

The earnest and thoughtful investigator uses spirit and reason to navigate, but the will to mystical justice makes one vulnerable.

If you get into the Black Lodge, you may not get back out. In wanting to believe, you risk your sanity.

When confronting crime, investigators come to understand crime's contours. You may come to resemble what you understand.

The sensitive are aware that oppressive culture may press anyone of us into the aggressor role just as easily as into the victim role.

This journey "instigated by the body of a dead girl" is not one that moves towards "existential knowledge," but rather spins within "the mess, the calamity, and the obscurity" of misogyny.[9]

82.

One afternoon Julie sat watching *Fire Walk with Me*. Her mother came in.

After watching with her daughter for a while she says, "This reminds me of childhood."

83.

A father farther gone	Cuts the path
Ties one on	towards home with a rage
Denial is not just a river	In a knot
It is a known unknown	That may be ourselves
Who opened the channel	who worked out the knots
And we've seen him before	We know we've see him

84.

Fuckfuckfuckfuckfuck.

Julie sits at her desk pulling her hair as she looks at her leaf-printed curtains, her potted geraniums, and beyond those, outside the window, the magnolia trees. Beyond that were the skater kids.

She can't see them, but can hear clattering boards and happy whoops.

Fuck.

85.

"It wasn't until the Young-Girl appeared that one could concretely experience what it means to 'fuck,' that is, to fuck someone without fucking anyone in particular. Because to fuck a being that is really so abstract, so utterly interchangeable, is to fuck in the absolute."[10]

86.

"The failure to see women as 'anyone in particular,' or as subjects endowed with their own ends, has allowed men to fuck women over for centuries."[11]

87.

The girls got where they felt almost able to grasp something real, but it made no difference. They still felt crazy.
Knowing was not enough.
Violence they had thought of as geographically specific proved miasmic. It floats free, everyone breathes in a bit.
Inhale, exhale. Just breathe.

88.

No one is to blame   Or blame goes
round and round   there is more than enough

89

Capitalists sign deals and order more factories built when they're offered attractive tax incentives.

They choose to expand in one city over another because goods can be shipped easy, because environmental laws are lax, because labor is cheap.

They hire young girls for their nimble hands and their docility.

The girls flock from all over because their local economies have collapsed. The local economies collapsed because of the factories.

This is mystical circle.

The factories cycle through time in three shifts. The girls come and go on slow busses first thing in the morning, late in the afternoon, and late at night.

90.

Deified	Backwards and forwards
Drawn onward	Both ways
Dad's friend's name is	always spelled
the same	B-o-b

91.

To destroy the girls' bodies, the murderer feeds them to his pigs. The pigs he in turn feeds to friends and social groups who host parties on his property. This is true.[12]

He sends leftovers to the rendering plant close to where he picked up the girls when they were alive.

The offal is rendered into an odorless semi-fluid.

After this cycle is reported in the news, officials try to calm the public, but ultimately they are forced to admit that yes, human remains were mixed with things people ate and used.[13] Little parts of women were mixed into lotions and lipsticks. But rest assured, the officials say, the risk to human health was very slight.[14]

92.

The Americas store violence in the bodies of those deemed Other.

When alive, border girls are treated as close to invisible.

They move around, doing industrial, domestic, or erotic labor. They turn the free-trade machine.

Sometimes border girls turn up dead, raped, and murdered. And when they twist into death, the threads slip into a larger narrative weave without snagging.

If the first push to bury their stories fails, they are posthumously shamed, then mourned, then fought about, then turned into spectacle saints. This is the script. Lives treated as just another hot piece.[15]

Mass grave media. Recycle, reuse, reduce, and renew.

93.

The girls are writing a play about the bloody spotting of systems, about all the panties ruined by the state.

94.

People argue that this is the system working.[16]
Leaders within these systems deny there is a system.

95.

Politicians say, "We should not view [the murder of women]
as a sociological phenomenon. We should view it as crime."[17]

They say such things as if there are bad actors but no plays.

They subscribe to a theory of government that does not
recognize society.

Meanwhile, the system continues "preparing for a still vaguer
scenario: black economies, offshore investments for laundering
money, and piracy." The system of globalization provides the
material support for drug trafficking while still hedging with the
sales of weapons to fight the trafficking.[18]

96.

Try to focus on	This
The positive	is still happening
I know you're	This
mad	is the moral
but this isn't	bankruptcy
helping	of capitalism
take a breath	as it instrumentalizes
darling	everyone

Your	Certain
dark	narratives
views	wouldn't get told
Alienates	if they weren't effective
your negative	wouldn't be effective
focus pushes	if they weren't told
men	again and again
I tell you	I didn't make these stories
sweetheart	but I am bound
because I care	to repeat

97.

Why are you so angry? What's the good? Say Juárez, the
Green River, Port Coquitlam . . . What can we do? Say the
Downtown Eastside, the highway of tears . . . I can't understand
what you want. Why these riddles? Say the names of the places
you haven't heard of yet. I am not speaking a knot. I am speaking
through cyclical nightmares.

98.

"The Young-Girl is an attempt to put a face—brave or not—
on the split subject of capital . . . As a figure for this foundational
self-alienation under capital, in which we, as women, are
simply place holders for their frustration and impotence,
the Young-Girl holds out the chance of turning this self-
estrangement against itself, not to beat a retreat to pre-modern
times, but to drive the logic to its breaking point. Endlessly

exposed, isolated, objectified, punished, fetishized, the Young-Girl stands for the universal prostitution of the human in the interest of objectified profit. She is the fold where 'crisis' opens onto everything capitalism withheld and withholds still, which ostensibly would include intimacy, proximity, community. The fold is inclusive of the negative reminder that capitalism has not fully penetrated and replicated in its own logic: filiation, the last traces of that mysterious thing Marx called 'species being,' creature warmth mixed with 'emotional' suffering, that irreducible nexus of potential-within-attachment that gets called love."[19]

99.

Men they love ask with straight faces, "Why are you so angry?" and the girls cannot answer without crying. They cannot answer, period. The girls try to describe the state of the state hidden in plain sight. "Who do you think is keeping you safe," men ask the girls rhetorically.

Meanwhile schools lay heavy stories of intrinsically hypocritical, indigestible violence of nation-building on undergrad shoulders. Students go home and end up screaming about the history of colonialism over Thanksgiving dinner.

After dessert, children and parents part ways. The kids get drunk and high with high school friends next to the Rio Grande, while back home their parents drink Jack Daniel's with ice as the news reports on the progress of the war. More Fort Bliss soldiers would be deployed next week to Middle Eastern desert towns.

100.

The commodity looks itself in the face. The commodity celebrates its becoming human in whore, says the theorist.

But he fails to think of her as also a being. He fails to see the whore commodity as a subject who claims humanity through her performance of what her customers fear to feel about our own markets.

She performs connection where there is a lack, and when men are violent they are violent against her humanity, which is theirs too.

101.

Witch which	is witch which
a witch	What should we say
before the fact?	after the act?
What should we	Just say
say	eye no
Just say	know
Say self	medication
meditation	profane illumination
for all those	girl things not
coping	coping
With trauma	without mechanisms
Self-care	Don't harm
Self-harm	Don't care

Whores always get what's coming. They see it from miles away.

102

This is about a world with 8 balls and .22 revolvers, hundred dollar bill beach towels and beer-mug-shaped lamps.

This is about a world with blunts and cell phones, cornmeal sacks and carved cottonwood roots, dildos and forties, gilt mirrors and machine-gun lighters, bouquets of panty roses and thoroughbred statuettes made of brass.

This is about a world with syringes filled with blue liquid and faux fur-lined handcuffs, night vision goggles and Spanish fly aphrodisiac, wallet photos of children in pink ruffles and velvet paintings of moonlit mountains. This is a world with things we have made.

This is about a world with aloe plants and borrowed dresses, colonized thought and cotton bales, coyotes and coyote myths and coyotes as a nickname for smugglers, Djarum black cigarettes and Dodge Ram Chargers. This is about a world with a psychic economy and *The Princess Bride* on network TV. A world of roses in rain and the Mother Peace tarot deck. A world with séances and the Trinity project, with Santa Teresa standing in for Juárez. A world with vegans and petty vandalism, the welcome wagon diner and water beds in mobile homes. A world of the world's largest enchilada at the Whole Enchilada Festival.

Our cities are mirrors facing one another to create a claustrophobic infinity. Stealth jets no one can see leave fantastical gaseous clouds over the changeable purple-blue-gray Oregon Mountains. So far so close.

This is about a world with ghost towns and company towns with cul-de-sacs and long paved roads, gas stations and churches, community theaters and shanty neighborhoods on their edges.

This is about a world with wild and domestic cats, pet parrots and wild roadrunners and doves and other birds. This is about a world with lonely, depressed horses in small pens and whole herds of wild horses running from helicopters.

This is about a world with mothers and women who remind you of your mother. About old lovers with long eyelashes and their beautiful new girlfriends who have fucked-up teeth.

This is about a world with neck- and bolo ties, dress shirts and tank tops and skydiving team sweatshirts in turquoise-blue.

This is about a world with tropical and boreal forests and trade wind and multi-latitude and rain-shadow deserts.

This is about a world with napalm and atomic bombs. A world with loaded handguns and razor blades hidden inside cheek pouches.

This is about a world with scripts for tragic plays and dictionaries for words like pratfall, charmeuse, and empathy, and more and more.

Girlhood is a stage. The desert is a stage. The landscape is as much an interior as it is a place you can get to by flying Southwest. It's cheap, but not easy. It will take all your modern courage.

If we can say the right words in the correct way, we can reorder the world. If we can reorganize our fragments we will begin to understand one another. Redeeming shitty experience is the option. This is the only experience we have.

After the world of the stage, we must make our entrance into this stage of the world.

105.

The stage goes dark and quiet. Girls appear
onstage Celine and Julie appear
to speak Onstage

Spirits possess the girls
Possession is nine-tenths of the law

Turn your head to the side to see we have parts but
the other, other side also are parts
not killers not victims not slow or methodical
not means to ends but but repetitive and messy
ends in and of themselves bodies emboldened
embodied

matter illegally crossing
matter acting out the violence of
matter objectifying beings

matter when you touch it
touches you back into being
into being matter touches you
all open

106.

Celine remembers a teacher saying, as she tried to get the class to look at art, Space is as real as what we call separate things. We're taught not to feel its embrace. We're taught to ignore our intertwining and overlapping. As you look, don't think about this, allow yourself to feel it.

A guy wearing headphones comes through the verdant park where Celine sits alone. He seems not to see her as he dances past an overflowing garbage can and a bunch of pink rose bushes.

You have to teach yourself how to feel the intimate connections between positive and negative again.

She feels a sensation she had felt before during sex, high on drugs, and when almost asleep. She looked as hard-soft as she could at the wet lacy patterns imprinted on the pavement from where leaves had been and gone.

She begins crying and keeps on for a long time.

107.

Darling Celine,

I am sitting below an apple tree in this strange city, listening to someone else's party on the other side of the fence. What a beautiful summer. There were so many times I wished you were here.

I keep remembering the last night I was in Cruces, when we said goodbye, goodbye, goodbye.

I keep imagining our time together as a collage. The performances, the parties, watching a movie on your couch while your parents had a dinner. I picture the time when you pulled a box of sparklers from your purse and we wrote a cursive message in explosive ink against the dark. Maybe it was because I was high, but I thought you could read what I wrote.

I think of the last time we said goodbye in my driveway and we hugged and kissed cheeks and said see you soon even though neither of us knew if that would be true.

The desert opened enough for the shape of your headlights to pass through. You drove away from my present tense.

Things have been so crazy that our separation has come to feel, if not right, then normal I guess. But tonight, in a tearful state I've been thinking how sorry I am that moment will be forever unrecorded—a nonexistent movie of you making swirls of fire between my house and the big dark. I don't know what you were writing, but I wanted you to know what I was.

Oh, Celine. I'm too young to feel such longing, but I do.

Elephant shoes sweet friend. Elephant shoes forever.

I miss you with my whole heart.

108.

This is a spell for getting out of girlhood alive.

Notes

1. Juárez has been talked about in business circles as a City of the Future in a positive way since the 1990s because of local government's adoption of free-trade-friendly policies. Many articles give a snapshot of the city in the 1990s as an industry-friendly darling (such as "Deep in the heart of NAFTA," *The Economist*, February 26, 1998). In 2007/08 the city was awarded the City of the Future award by *Foreign Direct Investment Magazine* (http://www.gdi-solutions.com/fdi/2007awards/Mexico/ciudad_juarez.htm). That same period marks a steep rise in the murder rate, from 320 in 2007 to 1,623 (or roughly 4.4 murders per day) in 2008 (http://fronteralist.org/category/murder-rate/) for a population of 1,300,000+ (http://www.borderplexalliance.org/regional-data/ciudad-juarez/market-overview/juarez-population).

   This is also an oblique reference to the important writings of Sergio González Rodríguez, Alicia Gaspar De Alba, Charles Bowden, and Alice Driver, among others. These scholars and journalists have all written important studies on the ways in which Juárez serves as a testing ground for neoliberalism, with brutal, life-destroying results. I am deeply indebted to their important work.

2. Jessica Benjamin, *The Bonds of Love* (New York: Pantheon, 1988), 76.

3. Sigmund Freud, *Civilization and Its Discontents*, trans. James Strachey (New York: W. W. Norton & Company, 2005), 26.

4. Benjamin, *The Bonds of Love*, 76.

5. Ken MacQueen, "Robert Pickton Murder Trial Begins," *The Canadian Encyclopedia*. http://www.thecanadianencyclopedia.ca/en/article/robert-pickton-murder-trial-begins/

6. "Black and White Lodge," *Twin Peaks*, Wikia. http://twinpeaks.wikia.com/wiki/Black_and_White_Lodge.

7. Neil Weiner and Sharon E. Robinson Kurpius, *Shattered Innocence* (New York: Routledge, 1995), 6.

8. Ibid.

9. Alice Bolin, "The Oldest Story: Toward a Theory of a Dead Girl Show," *The Los Angeles Review of Books*, April 28, 2014.

10. Tiqqun, *Preliminary Materials for a Theory of the Young-Girl*, trans. Ariana Reines (Cambridge: Semiotext(e), 2012), 94.

11. Moira Weigel and Mal Ahern, "Further Materials Toward a Theory of the Man-Child." *The New Inquiry*, July 9, 2013. http://thenewinquiry.com/essays/further-materials-toward-a-theory-of-the-man-child/

12. Charles Mudede, "Death Farm," *The Stranger*, October 30, 2003. http://www.thestranger.com/seattle/death-farm/Content?oid=16079

13. Petti Fong and Amy O'Brian, "Human remains suspected in Picton meat," *MissingPeople.net*, March 11, 2004. http://www.missingpeople.net/human_remains_suspected_in_pickt.htm

14. "When asked by the Crown if it were unusual to see big chunks, he said, 'They usually like to use every little piece of the meat that is on . . . from the animal because, you know it is money.' Unauthorized material," *CBC News*. http://www.cbc.ca/news/canada/unauthorized-material-could-be-dumped-at-rendering-plant-pickton-jury-hears-1.689012

15. Alicia Gaspar de Alba and Georgina Guzman, "Feminicidio: The 'Black Legend' of the Border," in *Making a Killing* (Austin: University of Texas Press, 2010).

16. In December 2014 the Inter-American Commission on Human Rights stated, "Disappearances and murders of Indigenous women in Canada are part of a broader pattern of violence and discrimination against Indigenous women in Canada." Samantha L. Dawson, "Seeking Justice for Cindy Gladue," *Maisonneuve*, April 2, 2015. http://maisonneuve.org/post/2015/04/2/seeking-justice-cindy-gladue/

17. "Native teen's slaying a 'crime,' not a 'sociological phenomenon,' Stephen Harper says," *thestar.com*, August 21, 2014. http://www.thestar.com/news/canada/2014/08/21/native_teens_slaying_a_crime_not_a_sociological_phenomenon_stephen_harper_says.html

18. "A Senate investigation found that HSBC was complicit in allowing Mexican drug cartels to launder billions of dollars through its US operations. The Senate report also says US regulators knew that the bank had a poor system to defend against laundering, but did nothing to demand improvement. While US forces were training and arming the Mexican military to fight cartels, US bankers were cashing in on cartel profits." Kristen Gwynne, "Mexican Drug War victims: US is Responsible," *Salon.com*, September 26, 2012. http://www.salon.com/2012/09/26/mexican_drug_war_victims_us_is_responsible/

19. Jaleh Mansoor, "Notes on Militant Folds: Against Weigel and Ahern's 'Further Materials Toward a Theory of the Man-Child." http://theclaudiusapp.com/5-mansoor.html

Acknowledgments

I wish to thank the following people for the many ways they offered support and inspiration: Geri Murphy, Bruce Blevins, Jessie Campbell, Rob Callaghan, Erin Robinsong, Stephanie Acosta, J. Soto, Rowan de Freitas, Kristi McCuire, Madeline Stack, Kevin Antranik Cassem, Jacob Wren, Zach Dodson, Chris Kraus, Ariana Reines, Jesse Ball, and Matthew Goulish.

Jay Millar, Hazel Millar, Ruth Zuchter, and Malcolm Sutton have been a dream to work with. Malcolm's sensitive editing has made this a stronger text than I could have made on my own. I am happy to have brought this book out with such generous and thoughtful individuals.

Over the course of writing this I had the good fortune to be an artist in residence with ACRE in Stuben and Sound Development City in Belgrade and Athens. I was also lucky to attend The Rhythm Party at Princeton University, perform at The Green Lantern and Links Hall in Chicago, as well as at the Fonderie Darling in Montreal. I taught at Abrons Art Center, served on the board at Wendy's Subway, and studied at Red Crow Yoga Shala, all in New York City. I have deep respect for the people who, under often challenging circumstances, keep these communities going. So much has been built on a foundation of their emotional, logistical, and financial backing. Time with these groups made life and art better.

Endless gratitude.

Colophon

Distributed in Canada by the Literary Press Group:
www.lpg.ca

Distributed in the United States by Small Press Distribution:
www.spdbooks.org

Shop online at www.bookthug.ca

Cover designed by Joni Murphy and Malcolm Sutton
Typeset in Parkinson Electra and Nitti Grotesk
Edited for the press by Malcolm Sutton
Copy edited by Ruth Zuchter

BOOK PRODUCTION WAR ECONOMY STANDARD